WHERE AM I?

Using the Book

This book can be read like a normal book. However, to make it more interesting, we have included a flap at the end. Use this flap to make a game out of the book.

Each page has four chunks of information on one place. Use the flap to show just one info block at a time, and try to identify the monument or city first and then the country. The fourth clue more or less tells you the place. Below the info blocks, you can see a picture connected to the place or monument and read some more about it.

Fold the sheet to show clues as shown in the figures.

Fold once to show the first clue. Able to guess the event and answer it right? Are you related to Newton or what? Get 20 points.

Fold again to show the second clue. Correct answer? Get 15 points. Your brain deserves to be kept in a museum.

Fold to show the third clue. A correct answer at this stage gets you 10. You may not be Newton but you are a close cousin.

No answers as yet? Fold again to show the fourth clue. This one was plain unlucky for you. Take 5, if you answer it here.

No answers? Guess what? You are actually the luckiest! You don't get any point, but you get to see the picture of the event and read some interesting tidbits about it.

Talk to Us

We invite readers to compile pieces of information in the style followed in this book. Try to keep some information that is interesting and seldom heard of, apart from the usual necessary information. Do not forget to include your source for the information. Send this to us with your name and address and we will include it in an upcoming edition of the book, with your name as a contributor.

So what are you waiting for? Get up and get cracking.

WHERE AM I?

Premlata
Salwan School
Rajinder Nagar, New Delhi

wisdom tree

This book is a compilation of facts and information from various sources. Care has been taken to verify the contents very thoroughly up to the time of publication. In case anyone has any query, clarification, complaint, or suggestion, please let us know, and we will immediately look into it. Also, in case anyone feels a credit is due, immediately write to us, and we will get back to you. Any infringement of copyright or trademark is not intended.

ISBN: 978-81-86685-80-8

First published 2004
Reprinted 2005, 2006, 2008, 2010, 2012, 2013

Published by
Wisdom Tree
4779/23, Ansari Road
Darya Ganj, New Delhi-110 002
Ph.: 011-23247966/67/68
wisdomtreebooks@gmail.com

Printed in India

Introduction

Quizzing is an art, where questions are the colours. And answers are like brushes with which you need to paint a beautiful, informative picture.

Most of the time, desire to know far exceeds the material available. And sometimes one feels lost in all kinds of materials available, when the need is specific. This book is designed to help satisfy the specific informatory needs regarding historic places of the world. I had the pleasure to write this fun-filled informative series.

In this competitive era, knowledge acquisition has no limitation. The process of inflow of information is continuous. But after a while, this entire business of information gathering becomes monotonous. This book is an effort towards making learning more innovative and exciting.

This book will serve like a whiff of fresh air that students, teachers or readers would like to have to develop a repository of information.

I hope you enjoy reading this book as also the others in the series. We would welcome your suggestions, if any.

Premlata

I am one of the most magnificent fort palaces in the world. For my inauguration, the main halls were covered with silk from China and velvet from Turkey. I am situated in the northeast corner of the original city of Shahjahanabad. My walls extend up to 2 km, and vary in height from 18 m on the riverside to 33 m on the cityside. The Mughal Emperor Shah Jahan started constructing me in 1638, and work was completed in 1648. I was attacked by the Persian Emperor, Nadir Shah in 1739.

I have a circumference of almost 2.4 km. My most beautiful section is the *Diwan-i-Khas*, which was the hall of private audience. The 90 x 67 ft *Diwan-i-Khas* is a pavilion of white marble supported by intricately carved pillars. Emperor Shah Jahan was so much in love with the beauty of this pavilion that he engraved on it: "If there is paradise on the face of this earth, it is this, it is this." There is an octagonal open space that was the market place—the *Chatta Chowk*. In the *Naubat Khana*, court musicians played music five times a day.

The *Diwan-i-Aam* is the hall of public audience. It is built of sandstone and covered with shell plaster polished to look like ivory. The hall is 80 x 40 ft and is sub-divided by columns. In an alcove in the back wall, the Emperor sat on a richly carved and inlaid marble platform. This platform once held the famous Peacock Throne, which, when it was plundered by Nadir Shah, was valued at six million sterling pounds. The marble canopy here is decorated with the most exquisite **pietra dura** work. Behind the *Diwan-i-Aam* are the women's quarters.

It was from here that the British sent the last Mughal ruler, Bahadur Shah Zafar, into exile to Burma, marking the end of the three-century-long Mughal rule. It was also from here that the first Prime Minister of India, Pandit Jawaharlal Nehru, announced that India was free from colonial rule. The fort is named after the redstone with which it is built. Entrance to the fort is through the imposing Lahore Gate, which as its name suggests faces Lahore, now in Pakistan.

The Red Fort, Delhi, India

The Red Fort also has a residence of the senior queens, the *Rang Mahal*. Constructed by Emperor Aurangzeb in 1662, Moti Masjid or the Pearl Mosque is built with highly polished marble. Other buildings in the Red Fort are the *Musamman Burg* (octagonal tower), *Khwabgah* (bedroom) and the *Hammam* (royal baths).

The Red Fort

I am built of 12,000 steel girders that are held together by 2,500,000 rivets. My functional elegance signifies industrial art, and conservative observers have never failed to pass sarcastic comments on my structure ever since I was completed in 1889. Till 1986, I was lighted up by external floodlights. Now, I glow from within at night with an internal system of illumination. The Prince of Wales, later King Edward VII of England, inaugurated me.

I was the tallest building in the world when I was built at a proud 300 m. I remained the highest monument in the world until the construction of New York's Chrysler Building in 1930. I was originally built as a temporary structure to commemorate the centenary of the French Revolution. I disgusted the author **Guy de Maupassant** so much that he left the city permanently to avoid looking at my 'metallic carcass'. However, I did win over the artists. **Seurat** and **Douanier Rousseau** were among the first to paint me.

I have three floors. The first is at 57 m, the second at 115 m, and the third at 276 m. The top of the aerial is 320 m above the ground. To reach my top, you need to climb up 1,652 steps. Believe me, it is worth it, for on a nice day, you can see not only my entire city but even the distant suburbs. If you get hungry while climbing, you will need to have a reservation and plenty of money to eat at my restaurant, the *Jules Verne*, on the second platform. The top platform has a bar and a souvenir shop.

My design was selected in a competition. Of the 700 proposals submitted, Gustave Eiffel's design was the said to be the best and was chosen. It was announced in 2003 that a copy of me measuring 22 m high will be used as a pole for an enormous 50 m Romanian flag to be hoisted up on the Bucharest Parliament rooftop. I am now a television transmitter. In fact it is my height that saved me from being torn down in 1909. My antenna was being used for telegraphy at that time.

Eiffel Tower,
Paris, France

It was constructed by Gustave Eiffel, an engineer who had experience of constructing high-level railway viaducts. Throughout its construction, the residents became convinced that it would collapse, and Gustave Eiffel had to personally assure them. From 1889 to 2002, the number of visitors have been 204,381,152. From 1910, it became part of the International Time Service, from 1918 of radio services and in 1957 of television programmes.

My chief architect was Sir William Empson, president of the British Institute of Architects. He based my design on Italian Renaissance architecture. Robert Lyons Serenoaks, the superintending architect, oversaw the day-to-day functioning. He was responsible for the execution of the project and sent photographs of the progress in my construction to Sir William every month. The total cost of my construction, one crore and five lakh rupees, was entirely from donations by Indians.

It is said that a goods train 17 miles long would have been required to bring the entire building material needed for building me. My total weight has been calculated to be around 80,300 tonnes and the marble required measured 16,080 cu ft. My foundation stone was laid by King George V in 1906 and the construction took 15 years. I was formally inaugurated on 28 December 1921 by King Edward VIII, who was still a prince then.

I have one of the best collections of oil paintings in India painted between the years 1770 and 1835 by some of the most distinguished European artists. The collection includes landscapes and cityscapes by Thomas and William Daniell, which are the most significant of their works in the world, and so are those by William Hodges, together with portraits and historical scenes by Tilly Kettle, Johann Zoffany, James Wales and Thamas Hickey. Sculptures include a bronze Victoria on her throne, a bronze Edward VII on his horse, and a marble Lord Curzon.

I was built under Lord Curzon, the then Viceroy of British India, who proposed the construction of a mausoleum in the centre of a garden in Queen Victoria's memory, after the death of the popular British monarch at the age of 94. He also proposed a museum in the same complex to house artifacts related to the British rule in India. The museum today has one of the best collections of artifacts to be found in any museum in India.

Victoria Memorial, West Bengal, India

The Victoria Memorial is located in the heart of Kolkata city, the capital of West Bengal, India. However, Curzon could not see its completion, as he had to leave for Britain soon after construction work began. The Calcutta Tercentenary Trust, founded in 1989, has raised and contributed substantial funds to Victoria Memorial.

I am a stone observatory built not only to verify astronomical observations but also to stimulate interest in astronomy. Huge astronomical instruments were built, following the style of an observatory at **Samarkand**, keeping in mind the rules of astronomy, the position of the equator, latitudes and longitudes. There are 14 major geometric devices for measuring time, predicting eclipses, tracking stars in their orbits, etc. Built of local stone and marble, each instrument carries an astronomical scale.

One of the instruments that I have is the *samrat yantra*. It is a huge triangle with a curved structure on both sides. Its face is lined with marble and tells the local time according to the shadow cast by the triangle. It can also be used to study the position of the sun and stars by using a metal rod. It is 90 ft high. There are etchings that were used to give the midday times of places such as Greenwich in England and Zurich in Switzerland, Notkey in Japan, and Seritchew Islands in the Pacific Ocean.

Another instrument is the *jaiprakash yantra*, which is in the form of two hemispherical bowls representing the spherical planets and stars. A vertical rod in the centre gives different positions of heavenly bodies. The measurements are etched on the marble lining. The *ram yantra* is in the form of a high cylinder surrounded by circular walls. The shadow of the sun on the vertical and horizontal marble gradations indicates the altitude and declination of stars and planets.

I was built by Maharaja Sawai Jai Singh II. I have four other brothers and sisters, who all look similar to me, in Delhi, Benares, Ujjain and Mathura, in India. The last no longer exists. I am the second built, and the largest. I was built in 1728 in the city founded by Jai Singh. Prior to this, astronomers in India, and also in other parts of Asia and Europe, relied on hand-held instruments of smaller proportions. The instruments that my siblings and I have are unique in the world.

Jantar Mantar in Jaipur, Rajasthan, India

Sawai Jai Singh was commissioned by Emperor Muhammad Shah to correct the existing astronomical tables and fix planetary positions anew. The first Jantar Mantar was built in Delhi in 1724. Today the instruments here cannot be relied upon to give the kind of accuracy that they gave then because of the growth of multistoreyed structures around it.

Samrat yantra

I am a palace with about 600 rooms and surrounded by 20 hectares of gardens. The Queen's Gallery inside me is dedicated to a permanent exhibition of items from the **Royal Collection** of art and treasures. Constructed 40 years ago on the bomb-damaged ruins of a former private chapel, the Gallery has been renovated. It was reopened by Queen Elizabeth on 21 May 2002 and is open to the public on a daily basis.

I face the Victoria Memorial, a statue of Queen Victoria. A statue of Nike, the ancient Greek goddess of victory, stands in front of me, also in memory of Queen Victoria. I have paintings by **Rembrandt, Rubens, Vermeer, Poussin,** Canaletto; sculpture by **Canova**; and some of the finest English and French furniture in the world. George III bought me in 1761 so that his wife, Queen Charlotte, could use me as a comfortable family home close to St James's Palace.

I have one of the finest working stables in the world, the Royal **Mews**. Visitors can see the work of the royal household department that provides road transport for the members of the royal family by both horse-drawn carriage and motor car. The Royal Mews has a permanent display of State vehicles, including the Gold State Coach used for **coronations**. The state rooms inside me are used extensively by the members of the royal family. They are lavishly furnished with some of the finest treasures from the Royal Collection.

The Duke of Buckingham and Normandy built me in 1703. I am the official residence in this city of the British monarch since Queen Victoria ascended the throne in 1837. Before this, St James's Palace used to be the official royal residence. I was redesigned by John Nash in 1825. The famous **Changing of Guard** ceremony takes place in my forecourt every day from April to September and every other day from October to March.

Buckingham Palace, London, United Kingdom

14 of George III's 15 children were born in Buckingham Palace when it was just a family house, known as the Queen's House. In 1762, the house was remodelled according to designs by Sir William Chambers, at a cost of £73,000. George IV, by the end of 1826, set about transforming the house into a palace with the assistance of his architect, John Nash.

I am a *gurudwara* named after Hari (God). Guru Arjan Sahib, the fifth Nanak, conceived the idea of creating a central place of worship for the Sikhs and he designed me himself. My architecture represents a unique harmony between the Muslim and the Hindu styles. It is often quoted that this architecture has created an independent Sikh school of architecture in the history of art in India.

The plan to excavate the holy tank that lay within my complex was chalked out by Guru Amardas Sahib, the third Nanak, but it was executed by Guru Ramdas Sahib under the supervision of Baba Budhaji. The land where I am situated was acquired by the earlier gurus, both on payment and free of cost from the *zamindars* of native villages. A plan to establish a town settlement was also made. The construction work on the tank and the town started simultaneously in 1570. The work on both projects was completed in AD 1577.

Guru Arjan Sahib got my foundation laid by a Muslim saint, Hazrat Mian Mirji, of Lahore on December 1588. The construction work was directly supervised by Guru Arjan Sahib himself, assisted by Baba Budhaji, Bhai Gurdasji, Bhai Sahloji and many others. I was completed in AD 1601. Guru Arjan Sahib installed a newly created *Guru Granth Sahib* inside me and appointed Baba Budhaji as the first reader of *Guru Granth Sahib*.

Also known as Sri Darbar Sahib, I am built on a 67 ft-square platform in the centre of the tank. I have a door on each of the four directions. My main structure is three-storeyed. My front, which faces a bridge, is decorated with repeated cusped arches and the roof of my first floor is 26 ft and 9 ins high. At the top of the first floor, a 4-ft high parapet rises on all the sides which has also four ***mamtees*** on the four corners. On the top of the central hall of my main sanctuary rises the third storey. It is a small square room and has three gates.

Golden Temple in Amritsar, Punjab, India

A regular recitation of *Guru Granth Sahib* is held in the room above the central hall. The *gurudwara* is covered with real gold. The smiths at the Golden Temple combine **gold leaf** with mercury and make many layers. In this way huge pieces of gold sheets are prepared. These are then attached to the building.

I am a unique and striking Buddhist monument in Southeast Asia. I was built during the time of the Sailendra dynasty who ruled over my country in the 8th and 9th centuries. I was constructed between AD 760-830. I resemble a pyramid with steps with a quadrangular base. On the top of my pyramid, I have ***stupas***. I have been built on and over a natural hill. I do not have a roof.

I have 460 panels on the top three **balustrades**, a third of which are based on the Buddhist story of *Gandavyuha*, which tells us about the pilgrimage of Sudhana who travelled all over India in search of truth. He met teachers, kings, queens, monks, nuns, goddesses, and *bodhisattvas* but none could tell him about the whole truth. I have 92 *dhyani* or meditative Buddhas around a central *stupa*. My central *stupa*, though 52 ft in diameter, has no image.

I am based on an island to which came Indian concepts, the Sanskrit language, and religions like Buddhism and Hinduism, through trading ships that carried priests. I am made up of 55,000 sq m of lava-rock. I am in the shape of a lotus. I am said to be a replica of the universe, divided into three levels: first is that in which man's desire is influenced by temptations; the second is that in which man still has desires but these are positive and the third is that in which man does not have worldly desires at all.

My name is an abbreviation for 'Bhumisan Brabadura', which translates into the 'mountain of accumulated virtues'. I lay forgotten until I was discovered in 1814 by Sir Thomas Stamford Raffles, the new British Governor of my country. Two hundred men under Raffles searched for me near the small village of Boro. The choking vegetation had to be burnt and tonnes of volcanic ash had to be cleared before they finally saw my stone figures.

Borobudur, Java, Indonesia

From geological studies, experts proved that the Borobudur area was at one time a big lake. It faces the east with a total of 1,460 panels. The temple walls measured a total of 2,500 sq m and were full of relief work. The *stupa* structure originated in India and the original purpose was for storing the cremation ash of Gautam Buddha and other holy Buddhist monks.

I am a hall in an ancient city founded in the 6th century BC by the **Achaemenids** as their capital. I was started by Xerxes and completed by his son Artaxerxes I. My country was built by Darius I the Great, who ruled between 521 and 485 BC. The dry climate has helped to preserve much of the architecture here. I am one of the forgotten wonders of the world.

My city has several buildings on a vast artificial stone terrace. The palaces were looted and burned by Alexander the Great in 331-330 BC My treasures are said to have been carried away by him on 20,000 mules and 5,000 camels. The city was first identified in 1620 but was not scientifically excavated until the 20th century, when an archaeological mission was sponsored by the Oriental Institute of the University of Chicago under Professor Ernst Herzfeld from 1931-1934, and Erich F. Schmidt from 1934-1939.

My ruins lie at the foot of *Kuh-i-Rahmat*, or 'mountain of mercy', in the plains of Marv Dasht. A wide double staircase, shallow enough for horses to climb, led to the top of the terrace of my city. The Gate of Xerxes welcomes people to the city, guarded by enormous carved stone bulls. The largest building is the *Apadana* or the Audience Hall, which could accommodate 10,000 people. Massive stone columns supported the roof, of which 36 were inside and another 36 supported verandahs on the three sides of the building. Only 13 columns are standing today.

I am the second largest building here and am also called the 'hundred-column hall'. I have eight stone doorways decorated with reliefs of throne scenes and the king. I have two colossal stone bulls on my north porch. In the beginning, I was used mainly as a receptiom hall for people from different regions of my empire. Later, I also acted as a storehouse and a showplace to display objects from the royal treasury. My city was called Parsa by the ancient Persians and it is known today in the country as *Takht-e-Jamshid* after a legendary king.

The Throne Hall of Persepolis, Iran

Persepolis is located 60 km northeast of Shiraz in Iran. The Shah of Iran, even in contemporary times, stored and exhibited royal treasures in galleries adjoining his throne hall in the Gulistan Palace at Tehran. The 100 columns of the throne room were made of wood but only their stone bases survive today. The palaces of Darius and Xerves also survive.

Pillars of Persepolis

I was originally called the Masjid-i-Jahanuma, or the 'mosque commanding a view of the world'. I am the last magnificient monument of the Mughal Emperor, Shah Jahan. I was built between 1644 and 1658 by 5,000 artisans. Every Friday, the Emperor would come from the fort opposite me to attend the communal prayers. I have three gates, and the largest and highest was on the east. This was reserved exclusively for the Emperor.

Broad flights of steps lead up to the imposing gateways in the north and the south. My main eastern entrance, earlier used by the emperors, remains closed on most days of the week. My main prayer hall lies on the westside. It has a series of high cusped arches and is topped with marble domes. It has a niche in a wall that shelters the prayer leader. Worshippers use this hall on most days. On Fridays and other holy days, my courtyard is full of devotees offering *namaaz*.

Apart from the three gateways, I have four towers and two minarets. I have been constructed of alternating vertical strips of red sandstone and white marble. In my centre is a large marble tank where people wash themselves before attending prayers. My **pulpit** is carved out of a single block of marble. My **minarets** are 130 ft high. On my north is a temple called Sri Digambar Jain Lal Mandir, which dates back to the time of Aurangzeb.

The Chawri Bazaar along my south-western side is one of the busiest trading centres of the city. In Marathi, *chawri* means a gathering place for trade and judicial business. This market was established during the reign of Shah Alam II. There are many old houses outside my grounds, called **havelis** and **kothis**. Near my north gate is a cupboard containing a collection of Muhammad's relics — Quran written on deerskin, a red beard-hair of the Prophet, his sandals and his footprint, embedded in a marble slab. On the east, I face the Red Fort.

Jama Masjid, Delhi, India

The mosque measures 65 m by 35 m, and the courtyard is a square of 100 m on each side. It is the largest mosque in India. It stands on the Bho Jhala, one of the two hills of the old Mughal capital city of Shahjahanabad. Other places of worship near it include Gauri Shankar Mandir, Gurudwara Sheesh Ganj and Sunehari Masjid.

I am a place of great historical and archaeological significance. Located on a hill, I am just 46 kms from the capital city of the centralmost state of India. I was rediscovered in 1818, and was not found to be in good shape. My restoration started in 1881 and finally between 1912 and 1919, I was fully repaired and restored. I am mentioned in the chronicles of Sri Lanka, which states that Mahendra, son of Ashoka, visited his mother at Vidisa, who brought him to see me. He stayed with me for a month.

The structures that I have are examples of the most organised construction of temples in the medieval period. I have magnificient gateways which add grace to my already existing beauty. My four gateways were constructed in 35 BC. These are called *torans* and are covered with explicit carvings, which depict scenes from the life of Buddha, and Jatakas — the stories relating to Buddha and his earlier births. Buddha is not represented directly but through symbols — lotus represents his birth, the tree his enlightenment, the wheel the title of his first sermon.

Even though I am related to Buddhism, I have more connections with Ashoka. He built my first *stupa* and put up many pillars here. I am most famous for the *stupas* which were built on the top of my hill. The purpose of my *stupas* was mainly religious and the most likely use was to keep relics. Some of my *stupas* thus contain relics of the disciples of Buddha. My *stupas* date back as early as the 3rd century and are built in stone blocks. Though most of my *stupas* are in ruins, three are intact and are of great archaeological value.

I have an Ashoka pillar on the southern entrance. I also had a huge bowl carved out of single rock where grain was stored. This grain was distributed among the monks who stayed with me. The Archaeological Survey of India maintains a museum on me that houses many items that were discovered during my excavation, including a sizeable collection of utensils and other items used by the monks.

Sanchi, Madhya Pradesh, India

Today in Sanchi, only the shaft of the Ashoka pillar stands. The lion crown, which is seen on the Indian currency, is kept in a museum. The crown has the famous four lions, which stand back to back. This figure was adopted as the national emblem of India. The Ashoka pillars are an excellent example of the Greco-Buddhist style and are known for their aesthetic proportions and exquisite structural balance.

I was initially an *ashram* founded in 1863 by poet Maharishi Devendranath Tagore. Located about 3 km from Bolpur railway station, a university was also founded inside me. Poush Utsav is a fair held from 7th-9th **Poush** (usually falls in December) every year to mark my foundation day. I get to enjoy tribal sports, dances and folk songs, including songs by Bauls, the wandering minstrels of Bengal, during this festival.

My university is probably the only one in the world where at least some classes are conducted under trees. I am a great centre of traditional and contemporary art. I have seen the growth and development of many renowned contemporary Indian artists from fields such as painting, sculpture, graphics, music, dance etc. on my grounds. I have several institutions — Patha Bhavan, Uttar Shiksha Sadana, Siksha Bhavan, Vidya Bhavan, Vinay Bhavan, Kala Bhavan, Sangeet Bhavan, Rabindra Bhavan, China Bhavan, Hindi Bhavan, etc.

In 1922, Rabindranath Tagore started a rural reconstruction centre 3 km away from me. In the Ballavpur forest, 4 km away from me, is a deer park. Nearby is Nonoor, famous for its Bakranath Shiva temple and the sulphur hot springs. During spring, my grounds become colourful not only with flowers but with the festivities of the festival of spring or Vasanta Utsav. Satyajit Ray and Indira Gandhi were two personalities among the many who studied with me.

Rabindra Janmotsav is celebrated in mid-April to mark the Bengali New Year and as well as Tagore's birth anniversary. My university is called Vishwa Bharti. I also have a museum called Vichittra and an art gallery called Nandan. My leather bags are famous and unique. My Uttarayan complex where Devendranath Tagore lived consists of several buildings, such as Udayana, Konark, Shyamali, Punascha and Udichi. These show the the architectural talents of Rathindranath Tagore.

Shantiniketan in West Bengal, India

An interesting feature about Shantiniketan is that sculptures, **frescoes**, **murals** and paintings of Rabindranath, Nandalal Bose, Ramkinkar, Binodbehari Mukhopadhyaya and others which adorn the campus.

Mahatma Gandhi and Tagore at Shantiniketan

I am a huge area with very low population density. One-fourth of my area is mountainous. My highest peak, Emi Koussi or Mount Koussi, is 3,415 m above sea level. Some of my peaks are covered by snow in the winter. My main mountain ranges are Hoggar, Azbine and Tibesti. I have the Atlantic Ocean on my west, the Atlas mountains and Mediterranean Sea on my north, the Red Sea and Egypt on my east.

The animals within me include: **gerbil**, **jerboa**, **cape hare**, **desert hedgehog**, **dorcas gazelle**, dama deer, anubis baboon, spotted hyena, common jackal, sand fox, Libyan striped weasel, and the slender mongoose. Only 2,00,000 km² are fertile oases, where dates, corn and fruits are grown. My oases are mostly depressions where water pops up from underground. During the Ice Age, about 10,000 years ago, I was savanna or grassland and animals like giraffes, lions, and elephants, used to roam within me.

1.5 million people live within me, most of these in Mauritania, Morocco and Algeria. The main groups of people are Bedouins, Sahrawis, Tuareg and Negroids. I get an annual rainfall of less than 5 ins each year. Night temperatures can be freezing while I am hotter than 54 degrees Celsius during daytme.

I am the world's largest desert. I am 9 million km² in size. My maximum length is 5,000 km from west to east. I keep growing. This spreading process started at least 8,000 years ago, when I was still fertile. The few fertile regions today are those fed by underground rivers and basins. Morocco and Tunisia are the most often-travelled countries within me.

Sahara Desert, North Africa

It covers the countries Mauritania, Morocco, Algeria, Tunisia, Libya, Egypt, Sudan, Chad, Niger and Mali of the African continent. The Sahara also contains over 300 species of migratory bird population. The desert can be divided into western Sahara, the central Ahaggar mountains, the Tibesti massif (a region of desert mountains and high plateaus), and the Libyan desert.

I am a temple in south India. I was originally built by Kulasekara Pandya, but it was the Nayaks, who ruled the city from the 16th-18th centuries and made me as beautiful as I am today. I have 12 towers or **gopurams**. The outer towers are the landmarks of my city, which is known as the 'Athens of the East'. The city was originally called Madhurapuram because honey or *madhu* is said to have dripped off the hair of **Lord Shiva** here.

I cover 6 hectares. Meenakshi Nayakkar **mandapam** is a big hall inside me consisting of 110 pillars. These have the figures of an animal called Yalli with a lion's body and an elephant's head. I have a golden lotus tank, Mariamman Teppakulum, for devotees to bathe. The area around my tank was the meeting place of the Tamil Sangam — the ancient academy of poets. The annual Float Festival is held in my tank each January. The Shiva Meenakshi idols are taken out of my temples and are floated on decorated rafts.

My most wonderful structure is the thousand-pillar *mandapam* with 985 pillars. Each pillar is a magnificient monument of Dravidan sculpture. There is a Temple Art Museum in this hall where you can see icons, photographs, drawings, etc. Just outside this hall are the musical pillars. Each pillar when struck, produces a different musical note. The pillars of the Vasantha *mandapam* contain elaborate sculptures of Shiva and Meenakshi, as well as Nayak kings and their consorts. This is also called the Pudhu *mandapam*.

I am dedicated to Meenakshi, Lord Shiva's consort. I have an *oonjal* (swing) *mandapam* on the western side of my tank. Every Friday, the golden idols of Meenakshi and Sundareswarar are seated on the swing in the *oonjal mandapam* and hymns are sung as the deities gaily swing to and fro. The parrots in the Kilikoontu *mandapam* have been trained to repeat Meenakshi's name. During the Chitirai Festival in April/May, the idols are taken around on their chariots to celebrate the anniversary of the divine marriage.

Meenakshi temple in Madurai, Tamil Nadu, India

Legend says that Meenakshi came out from a sacred fire and was adopted by Malayadwaja Pandya, the king of Madurai. She had three breasts and a lovely voice. It was said the third breast would disappear when she met her soulmate. This happened when she met Shiva. After ruling over the Pandya kingdom for a while, they settled in the Madurai temple. Only Hindus are allowed inside the main shrine of the Shiva temple and only Hindu women in the Meenakshi temple.

I am a temple. My construction was supervised by Pheidias, the famous Athenian sculptor, while Iktinos and Kallikrates were the architects. I am built in the **Doric order** and almost exclusively of **Pentelic marble**. I have a rectangular floor plan with a series of low steps on every side. 136 columns surround me on the periphery. Each of my entrances has an additional six columns in front of it.

The larger of my two interior rooms, the *naos*, had a famous **chryselephantine** cult statue of Athena, made by Pheidias. I have relief work on the exterior, which depicts the procession of the Panathenaea, the most formal religious festival of ancient Athens. The scene runs along all my four sides and includes the figures of gods, beasts and of some 360 humans.

I was, turn by turn, converted into a Byzantine church, then a Latin church and subsequently a Muslim mosque. I myself was built replacing two earlier temples of Athena. When the Venetians, under Admiral Morosini, sieged the area I am in, in 1687, one of the Venetian bombs fell on me. This explosion destroyed a great part of me. I was till then in quite good condition.

I am the most important monument of the ancient Greek civilisation and I still remain its international symbol. I am dedicated to Athena Parthenos, the goddess of Athens. I was built between 447-438 BC. The work on the structural decorations continued till 432 BC. When work began on me, the Athenian Empire was at the height of its power.

Parthenon, Athens, Greece

In the beginning of the 19th century, the British ambassador in Constantinople, Lord Elgin, took away the greatest parts of the sculptural decoration of the monument, transferred them to England and sold them to the British Museum, where they are still exhibited. They are one of the most significant collections of the museum.

I am one of the most important landmarks of this capital city. I am a museum located on Marylebone Road and a visit to me is a great experience. Nearby is a planetarium, Regent Park, a zoo and Oxford Street. I was started by Marie Grosholz, whose name later changed into the name that you know me by today. After marriage, for the next 33 years, she moved me from town to town as a travelling showperson.

I first started as an exhibition. In 1835, Marie settled into a permanent home. She died in 1850. Her grandson, Joseph Randall, moved me to my present site. I was once damaged by fire and later by a bombing raid during Second World War, but I continued to grow and be successful. I am one of the city's top tourist attractions today. I make it possible for you to have a photo taken with a favourite star, personality, etc.

I have a Chamber of Horrors, where there is a **guillotine** (with its original blade from France), an **electric chair** and a real gallows from **Hertford Gaol**. There are also displays of notorious murderers showing how they committed their crimes. Besides this, there is the Garden Party, 200 Years, Superstars & Legends, the magnificent Grand Hall, and The Spirit of London. Hollywood legends and superstars include stars from Marlon Brando to Slyvester Stallone.

I have one of the world's greatest waxwork collection. The oldest waxwork that I have, Sleeping Beauty, dates back to 1765. Amitabh Bachchan became the first Indian film star to be added to my collection. For each wax model, over 900 kg of wax is required and a time period of six months, and approximately $45,000. Over two million people from all over the world visit me each year, making me one of the country's most popular attractions.

Madame Tussaud's Wax Museum, London, United Kingdom

After arriving from France in 1802, Madame Tussaud toured England with 35 wax models before setting up in Baker Street in 1835. When she died in 1850, her son continued the exhibition. The wax figures keep growing every year. Its branch was built in New York in 2000.

Amitabh Bachchan's wax statue

I am a treasure-house of marine life. I have within me 1,500 species of fish and 4,000 types of **mollusc**. I am also the habitat of endangered species such as the *dugong* (sea cow) and the large green turtle. A part of me has also been a marine park since 1975 and I am the largest marine protected area in the world. My marine park is 3,48,700 sq km in area and 2,300 km long approximately.

I have about 618 continental islands, which were once part of the mainland. These include Green Island, which has white sandy beaches, glass-bottom boats and an underwater observatory. Fitzroy Island with a lush rain-forest is almost completely surrounded by me. Michaelmas Cay is a unique nesting place for thousands of seabirds. Hinchinbrook Island is the world's largest island National Park, uninhabited except for a luxury resort.

I am made up of a thin layer of living animals called polyps, which secrete a chalky, limestone skeleton as they grow. These colonies grow and I too grow as the polyps divide and multiply. I catch planktons with my tentacles for food and also relish the single-celled **algae** called *zooxanthellae* living inside me. I use the nutrients prepared by the zooxanthellae through photosynthesis. No wonder that I grow three times faster when there are zooxanthellae inside me.

I am the largest coral reef in the world. Of the 400 types of coral that I have, the staghorn is one of the most common. I am actually a collection of over 2,900 reefs which includes 760 **fringing reefs** and 300 **coral cays**. I also have 500 species of seaweed, 215 species of birds, 16 species of sea snake and six species of sea turtle.

The Great Barrier Reef, Australia

The Great Barrier Reef with its coral reefs is a wonderland of colour and beauty, a site of remarkable variety on the north-east coast of Australia. Encrusting red algae form the purplish red algal rim that is one of the reef's characteristic features

Just one of the 1,500 varieties of fish found here

My construction began in 1631 and I took 22 years to complete. Twenty thousand people worked on me. The material was brought in from all over India and Central Asia and it took a fleet of 1,000 elephants to transport it to my site. I was designed by the Iranian architect Ustad Isa. I have a high base of red sandstone, which is topped by a huge white marble terrace. On this terrace my main body rests with a dome and four tapering minarets.

My Emperor was imprisoned in a Fort for eight years towards the end of his life by his son. During his imprisonment, I saw him every day, looking at me from a small window. He was probably remembering his wife who lies within me, but I couldn't help feeling that he was losing himself in my beauty. I am said to be a dream in milky white **pristine** marble. People come to look at me from all across the world. Many have written poems on me. I am one of the most photographed monuments of the world.

I stand on the bank of River Yamuna. I was built by the fifth Mughal Emperor in 1631. Eveything inside me is beautifully coordinated and it is all symmetrical except for the the casket of the Emperor who built me. I was to have a twin made of black marble in which this casket was to be laid but as this could not be done, the Emperor was laid beside his queen, for whom I was built. In my heart lies the jewel-inlaid tomb of the queen.

My Emperor's name is Shah Jahan. He built me in memory of his wife Arjumand Banu, also called Mumtaz Mahal, who died after 18 years of marriage. I have many beautiful **ancillary** structures, mosques and a well-laid out garden. I stand quite alone on the bank of the river. As the colour of the day and seasons change, you will notice that I too change, just like the different moods of a woman. I appear pink in the morning, milky white in the evening and golden when the moon shines. I am said to look my most beautiful on a full moon night.

Taj Mahal, Uttar Pradesh, India

The origin of the name of the monument is not clear. Court historians from Shah Jahan's time only call it the *rauza* (tomb) of Mumtaz Mahal. It is generally believed that Taj Mahal (translated as either 'crown palace' or 'crown of the palace') is an abbreviated version of her name, Mumtaz Mahal.

I can be called a magical city. Initially, the man who planned me thought of building me on 8 acres of land next to his studios. This was soon realised to be too small, and the plans were kept on hold. As he could not make financiers believe in the idea strongly enough, the man made television shows with the name by which I am known today. One interesting thing about me is that you do not find chewing gum and alcohol inside my boundaries.

I was finally inaugurated on 17 July 1955. Six thousand invitations to the grand opening were sent and over 28,000 ticket holders stormed into me. Most of the tickets were counterfeit. The city I am in considers me today as much a part of it as the Pacific Ocean and the Redwood Forests. I cost $17,000,000 to build.

The land that I am in now used to be just 180 acres of orange groves and walnut trees. My designer and maker had a plan for me that no one else had ever tried out before. Within me I have wild animals (animated but not real), Mississippi paddle ships, and castles. I have five uniquely different lands inside me: Main Street, Adventureland, Frontierland, Fantasyland, and Tomorrowland. A 20-ft earth wall was constructed around me.

Every building, lamp-post, store, trash can and so on is based on paintings, drawings. I see flying elephants and giant teacups, a fairy-tale castle, moon rockets, and railways inside me. You can see Ariel the Mermaid, experience how it feels being tiny, meet Alladin and Jasmine, drive fantasy cars on highways of the future, land on Tom Sawyer's island, meet Winnie the Pooh, Mickey and Donald, explore Tarzan's treehouse, fly with Peter Pan, and what not...

Disneyland, California, USA

Walt Disney would frequently stoop down while looking at a partially constructed building to see how children would see things. Disneyland's address, 1313 Harbor Boulevard, was given by Disney because there was nothing around that place for an official address. He chose this either to signify Mickey Mouse (M is the 13th letter of the alphabet) or as a double unlucky number to ridicule the people who told him he would fail.

The castle at Disneyland

We are caves that lie in the Chamadari hills. We represent 300 years of Hinduism, Buddhism, and Jainism. We were carved during AD 350-700. When you look at us, you will see us as an irregular ridge of rock raised vertically from the ground. Out of the 34 of us, 16 caves are the oldest and were carved in the 5th century. Mural paintings are found in five caves, but remain somewhat intact only in the Kailashnath temple.

Most of the older 16 caves are **viharas** but Cave No. 10 is a *chaitya*. These caves are called the 'Vishvakarma' caves. There are sculptures of couples along the balustrade. Cave 32 is dedicated to Jainism and is a beautiful shrine with exquisite carvings of a lotus flower on the ceiling and an imposing *yakshi* seated on her lion under a mango tree laden with fruit. The ceiling of this double-storeyed cave is also decorated with paintings.

Our monuments were chiefly patronised by the Chalukya-Rashtrakuta rulers (7th-10th century AD). Only 12 caves are Buddhist, but even these caves incorporate Hindu and Jain themes. The Buddhists believe that Buddha returns after every 5,000 years and Cave 12 has seven images of Buddha depicting his seven incarnations. We run north-south and the late afternoon sun makes us glow with beauty.

Our Hindu caves are completely different from the Jain and Buddhist temples in style and execution skills. Cave 14, also known as Kailashnath temple, depicts Lord Shiva as 'the destroyer'. It was built in the 16th century and was intended to depict Mount Kailash from a single stone. To make it, 2,00,000 tonnes of rock had to be removed and it took 100 years to be completed. The Ramesvara cave has figurines of river goddesses adorning its entrance. The Dumar Lena cave is also dedicated to Lord Shiva

---

Ellora Caves, Maharashtra, India

The mural paintings here were done in two series — the first set was at the time of carving the caves and another set was done much later. The earlier paintings show **Vishnu** and **Lakshmi** borne through the clouds by ***garuda***, with clouds in the background. Every year in the third week of March, the Ellora Festival of Classical Dance and Music takes place at the caves.

I am a city full of ruins and temples. The Virupaksha temple at my western end is one of my earliest structures. The main shrine here is dedicated to Virupaksha, a form of Lord Vishnu. On the south of the temple is the Hemakutta hills with many ruins, including Jain temples and a 6.7 m monolithic structure of **Narasimha**. A gigantic **Shivalinga** is located next to the Narasimha figure. It is 3 m high and stands permanently in water that comes through an ancient channel.

I also have the ruins of the Vithala temple, which is a World Heritage monument. The outer pillars of this temple are known as musical pillars, as they echo when tapped. This practice is not allowed nowadays. The temple also has a chariot with an image of *garuda*, the bird that carried Vishnu. If you look at the ruins of the Tirvengalanatha temple, you can see some sculptures in the columns inside the open halls near the main gateway.

I have a Lotus Mahal, which is a graceful two-storeyed pavilion located in the *zenana* enclosure style. The palace has a mix of Hindu and Islamic styles of architecture. My Virupaksha Bazaar is a 32 m wide and 728 m long street that runs between the Virupaksha temple and the foot of the Matanga hill and is the longest street laid out by the Vijayanagara kings.

I was the capital city of the Vijayanagar Empire. I was founded in the middle of 14th century by two princes, Hakka and Bukka of the Vijayanagar Empire. I was raided, looted and burnt in AD 1565, after the armies of Muslim sultanates of the Deccan defeated Vijayanagar. My elephant stables are famous.

Hampi, Near Bangalore, Karnataka, India

Hampi has a Queen's Bath situated in the citadel area, south of the Hazaara Rama temple. It is a large square structure, with a very plain exterior and a very elaborately decorated interior. The main entrance to Hampi is a gateway called Singaradu Hebbagilu. Located behind the elephant stables, this is one of the oldest and most massive of the gateways in the city.

I am a 2,000-year old city. I have within me temples, theatres, monasteries, houses and roads. I have over 800 monuments, mostly carved from sandstone by Nabataeans, a tribe of pre-Roman Arabs who dominated the region around the 6th century BC. I was rediscovered in 1812 by the Swiss explorer, John Ludwig Burckhardt, who heard about me from the Bedouins. Some workshops for metal and stone have been also been found inside me.

You enter me through a long winding path between overhanging cliffs, called *Siq*. My most magnificent and stunning monument is the *El Khazneh* or the treasury. Some believe that it is a tomb. It is 40 m high and about 30 x 30 m wide, depicting mythological figures. It is also the best preserved of all the monuments. It is now famous from its appearance in many movies, including *Indiana Jones and the Last Crusade.*

The Nabataean people had great wealth from their control of the trade routes that connected China, India and southern Arabia with Anatolia, Greece, Rome, Egypt and Syria. My rock-carved theatre could seat about 2,000 people. **Facades** of early tombs were partly cut away during the construction of the theatre. The walls of the *Siq* are lined with channels to carry drinking water to the city. A dam then diverted a stream through a tunnel to prevent it from flooding the *Siq*.

The huge columns of the treasury are graceful to say the least. Above the doorway is a figure of Al-Uzza, a great goddess, holding a **cornucopia**. My Urn Tomb is also well known. It has a courtyard with columns on two sides. High up, there are three niches leading to small burial chambers. I am entirely carved into the red sandstone cliffs and flourished for over 400 years, until occupied by Roman legions of Emperor Trajan in AD 106. My name literally means 'rock'. I am a UNESCO World Heritage Site.

Petra, the rock-carved city, Jordan

After the Romans came into Petra, its position as a commercial centre lowered. Next it was occupied by the Byzantines. Earthquakes and economic strains slowly ruined it. The fantastic hydraulic system too fell into ruin. Large rock-carved cisterns that stored water piped from quite a distance away are seen even today.

Treasury at Petra

I am a natural wonder of the new world. If you want to describe me in simple words, you will perhaps say that I am just a great chasm through the rocks of a plateau with good views. However, as you sit inside me, and look around you, you will realise that I am much more than that. I can teach you humility through my rocks carved over millennia, by my vastness and by the solitude I provide you.

I am also a National Park. I have an average of five million visitors a year. My south rim averages 2,134 m above sea level. The desert-view drive will lead you along this rim to desert view — the east entrance to the park. Hermit Road follows the rim for 13 km west to Hermits Rest. A hiking trail, known as the Rim Trail, follows the rim from Pipe Creek Vista to Hermits Rest.

Over 250 people are rescued from my depths each year. My north rim is over 2,438 m above sea level. Point Imperial, the highest point on the north rim at 8,803 ft, overlooks the Painted Desert. I have an area of more than 1.2 million acres but most of my area is inaccessible due to the predominance of cliffs. My wildlife includes my country's national symbol, the bald eagle, and others like the California condor, the golden eagle, desert bighorn sheep, etc.

River Colorado flows along my bottom. Lee's Ferry marks my official starting point. Outside my boundary, on the southern side of the river, is the Havasupai Indian Reservation administered by the Havasupai Indian tribe. I am a part of the Yellowstone National Park. I was designated a World Heritage Site on 26 October 1979.

Grand Canyon, Arizona, United States of America

Environmental issues at Grand Canyon include air quality, fire management, the impact of increased tourists and endangered species. The flow of River Colorado through Grand Canyon is controlled by the release of water from Glen Canyon Dam, 24 km upstream from the park boundary at Lee's Ferry.

I am a monument that towers over the city I am built in. In my complex also lies the Quwwatu'l-Islam Mosque and Alai Darwaza. There is a legend that I was built by Prithviraj, the last Chauhan king of Delhi, so that his daughter could see the Yamuna, from my top as part of her daily worship. My entire architecture, however, is Islamic and hence you can ignore this legend.

Originally I had only four storeys faced with red and buff sandstone. If you take a look at the **Nagari** and Persian inscriptions on me, you will read that I was probably damaged twice by lightning, in 1326 and 1368. My red sandstone tower is covered with beautiful carvings and inscribed with verses from the Quran. My mosque was constructed by Qutub-ud-din Aibak, the first ruler of the Slave Dynasty, using the materials and masonry of the remains of Hindu temples and architecture.

In the courtyard of my Quwwatu'l-Islam Mosque stands a famous iron pillar. It has a Sanskrit inscription in the script used during the Gupta era. I heard that it was brought to me by Anangpal, the Tomar king. If you have any fond wishes or desires, you just have to encircle your arms around this pillar and wish. All that you want will come true. However, the people who look after me do not think this is a very good idea and hence they do not allow people to do this any more. This pillar shows no rust despite its age.

I am still the highest stone tower in India, what if I am old now. I am also considered one of the finest Islamic structures and am synonymous with India's capital city. Sultan Qutub-ud-din Aibak started building me, and his son-in-law Iltutmish, completed me as I am today. In 1199, when I was started, Qutub-ud-Din either intended me to be a victory tower or a minaret to my mosque. From a base of 14.32 m, I taper to 2.75 m at a height of 72.5 m. My height is enough reason to tell you why it took two decades to complete me.

Qutub Minar, New Delhi, India

The Qutub Minar still remains a superb spectacle of Afghan architecture. One has to climb 379 steps to get to the top. The *minar* is said to have been built to celebrate the victory of Mohammed Ghori, the invader from Afghanistan, over the Rajputs in 1192. Firozeshah Tughlak restored and added two more floors, in which he introduced white marble.

Anchit

I stand in the heart of the city built by Quli Qutub Shah, in 1591. I am often called the 'Arc de triomphe of the East'. I am considered to be a masterpiece of the Qutub Shahi period. This city that I am in was established because there was inadequacy of water and frequent epidemics of plague and cholera raged in the old capital. I was built at the centre of the city with four great roads going out in four directions.

I was built with granite and lime-mortar. I am a blend of Cazia and Islamic style of architecture and depict the Indo-Saracenic tradition. This is a blend of the Hindu and the Muslim traditions, which has given rise to the rich Deccan culture. There are 45 prayer spaces within me with a large open space in front for Friday prayers. To the east of this space is a verandah with a large open arch in the centre, flanked by smaller ones on both sides.

My base is a square, each side of which is 20 m long, while my four arches are 11 m wide and rise 20 m from the plinth. The four-storeyed minarets rise 20 m from my roof and measure 24 m from the plinth. The western section of my roof contains a mosque, and people say that this is amongst the finest built by the Qutub Shahi artisans.

I get my name from my four intricately carved minarets or *minars*. I am located amidst the colourful shops of Lad Bazaar with its glittering traditional bangles. Sarojini Naidu had once written a poem on the bangle-sellers of my city. I am enormous in size and despite being 400-years old, I am still as charming and youthful as ever. At night, all lighted up, I am at my most beautiful.

Charminar in Hyderabad, Andhra Pradesh, India

Inside the four-storeyed minarets are spiral stairways of 149 steps leading to the top. Apart from the main arches on the four sides, above each arch are horizontal arrays of arches. Again, flanking each arch are four arched and **trellised** windows, one above the other. The four main arches have 32 such windows.

I am an architectural wonder. It is said that to make me, workers re-enacted a labour worthy of Hercules: they shifted the course of the seventh biggest river in the world and removed more than 50 million tonnes of earth and rock. My powerhouse is my main strength. My generating capacity is 12,000,000 kilowatts (kW). From 2004 onwards, my installed capacity increased to 14,000,000 kW.

I consist of a series of various types of dams and measure a total distance of 7,744 m with a crest elevation of 225 m. My main dam is of the hollow gravity type. The other kinds of dams that make me up include wing dams, cardhfill diges, rockfill dams and earthfill dams. I am built on the Upper Paraná river. I was built from 1975-1991 in a binational development. In 2000, I produced 93.4 billion kilowatt-hours (kWh) of electricity, the highest production of a power plant in the world.

The amount of iron and steel used in building me would be enough to build 380 Eiffel Towers, and the amount of concrete used is 15 times the volume used to build the tunnel between France and England. I provide the cheapest electric power in South America. My reservoir flooded 1,350 sq kms, drowning Sete Quedas, a waterfall more impressive than Iguazú, which is nearby.

I am the world's largest hydroelectricity project. I am also a major tourism attraction and have welcomed over nine million visitors from 162 countries. 30,000 people were involved in my construction. 18 is my favourite number: I have 18 generators, I took 18 years to finish and it took $18 billion to build me. Since 2004 onwards, I have had 20 generating units.

Itaipú Dam, Paraguay and Brazil

Itaipú Dam supplies 91 per cent of Paraguay's electricity, plus 26 per cent of Brazil's. The river it is on runs between Argentina and Brazil. *Itaipu* is a **Guarani** word for 'the singing stone'. It is named after a rock island that was located where the dam is today. When water splashed on the island, there was a noise and hence the name: singing rock.

I am the massive tomb of a king. There was marble covering my exterior but that has been eroded over time. My top platform is 10 m square. My base is 754 ft and covers 13 acres. My original entrance was about 15 m higher than the entrance that is used today. Some people say that I was built by peasants who may have been paid with food for their labour. The floods in the river that flows quite near is believed to have aided in moving the stones right up to where I stand.

At my base, on the southern side, you can find boat pits and a museum. Five boat pits were discovered in 1982. One boat can be seen at the museum. The boat is encased in stones and has no nails. It is held together with ropes and pegs and looks almost as good as new. These boats are said to take the soul of the dead in the journey after life. Inside me is also the queen's chamber, which was never used. The floor in this room was never polished and is still rough.

To my west is the royal cemetery. A 4,600-year-old female mummy had been discovered at this site. The king whose tomb I am was called Khufu. I was raided and plundered before archaeologists discovered me. The walls of the king's chamber are made of pink **Aswan granite**. Inside this chamber is the very large **sarcophagus** made of red Aswan granite. It must have been placed inside the chamber while I was being built because it is too large to bring inside later.

I am the largest and the oldest of the structures of Giza. I am most probably built between 2589-2566 BC. Over 2,300,000 blocks of stone with an average weight of 2.5 tonnes her each have been used to build me. The total weight would have been 6,000,000 tonnes and a height of 482 ft. I haven't counted but it possibly took 30 years and 1,00,000 slaves to have built me. There was also a mortuary temple near me, of which little remains today.

Pyramid of Cheops, Giza, Eqypt

There are ventilating shafts in the pyramid. These may not be actually ventilation shafts, but may have a more religious significance. Three small pyramids stand to the east of Cheops' pyramid. These are thought to have been for his sister, Merites, who was also his wife, and possibly two other queens.

I am a magnificent palace built by Nawab Vikar-ul-Ulmara, the then Prime Minister of the state. I was later gifted to Mehboob Ali Khan, the sixth Nizam of the kingdom. My name means 'star of heaven'. I am a rare blend of Italian and Tudor architecture, and was designed by an Italian architect.

My shape resembles a scorpion with two stings spread out as wings in the north. I have priceless collections of paintings, statues and English furniture. I also have the largest **Venetian chandeliers**. My glass-stained windows throw colours into the rooms. My walls have murals painted on them and are so beautiful that you can lose yourself. The staircase leading to my upper floor has carved balustrades and marble figures as supports.

I have a jade collection that is considered to be unique in the world. My walnut carved roof is a replica of the one at Windsor Castle. My library has one of the finest collections of the Quran. If you are hungry, enter my dining room. It is so huge that at a time it can accommodate 100 guests. I have one of the largest switchboards in India. It takes six months to clean a 138-arm **Osler chandelier** and I have 40 such chandeliers adorning the halls.

I am located on a hill above 200 ft. It took nine long years to complete my construction. I am entirely made with Italian marble and cover a total area of 9,39,712 sq m. I am 5 km to the south of the Charminar. I was purchased by Nizam VI in 1897 and used as a royal guesthouse. I look over the entire city and my guests were all treated to royal splendour.

Falaknuma Palace, Hyderabad, Andhra Pradesh, India

It is now the private property of Wala Shah Nawab Mukarram Jah Bahadur, grandson of the seventh Nizam. Prior permission is required to visit this palace. A visit to the Falaknuma palace is an awe-inspiring experience. It has one of the most lavishly decorated interiors.

I am a church built in 1661. My architectural style is **Baroque** and **Manuline**. I am built of **laterite** blocks and am plastered with lime. I face west and have three chapels, a choir, two altars in the **transept** and a main altar. To the north of my main altar is a **belfry** and a **sacristy**. A convent, which was an annexe to me, is now the archaeological museum.

Eight **Franciscan friars** on their arrival in 1517 in the country got a few houses from the then Governor. These houses belonged to a deceased ***thanedar***. Persevering and persistent, they constructed a small chapel with three altars and a choir. This can be said to be my origin. A **consecrated** church was built in 1521 and was later pulled down. I was then built in the same spot in 1661 in my present form, with the entrance of the earlier church.

My exterior is Tuscan while the main entrance is in Manuline style. My main altar is Baroque with Corinthian features. The inside walls, separating the chapels and supporting the gallery on top, have frescoes with intricate floral designs. In a niche on my facade stands a statue of **Our Lady of Miracles** brought from Jaffna in Sri Lanka.

On a pedestal inside me stands a wooden statue of St. Francis of Assisi bearing the **insignia** of the Franciscans. Beneath a ribbed vault with frescoes showing floral decorations is the main altar. My main altar is gilded and has a richly carved niche with a **tabernacle** supported by four **evangelists**.

Church of St. Francis of Assisi in Panjim, Old Goa, India

In the main altar, apart from the statue of St. Francis, there is an equally large statue of Jesus on the cross. Beneath the two figures are inscribed the three vows of the saint — poverty, humility and obedience. On either side of the main altar are beautiful large paintings on wood, depicting scenes from the life of St. Francis of Assisi.

I am a modern wonder of the world. I was built in 1976 by a railway company to demonstrate the strength of my country's industry. Each year, approximately two million people visit me for the view I offer. I cost the company $63 million and 1,537 workers were employed in my construction. In 1995, I was classified as one of the Seven Wonders of the Modern World by the American Society of Civil Engineers.

I have a revolving restaurant at 1,150 ft, and an observation gallery at 1,465 ft. Tourists move up in six glass-fronted, high-speed elevators at a speed of 22 ft/sec. The 1,136 ft level is reached in 58 sec. I have a low centre of gravity and that is how I get my stability. This low centre of gravity is due to a massive buried foundation beneath the visible structure. My base is made up of 7,034 cu m of concrete, 500 tonnes of reinforced steel and 40 tonnes of tensioning cable. My total weight is 1,30,000 tonnes.

In the 1960s, the capital city of my country saw many skyscrapers arising. These new buildings caused serious problems in communication through phone or radio. I was built with microwave receptors at 1,109 ft and 1,815 ft with 5 ins antennae, and I quickly solved the communication problem. I am thus an important telecommunications hub. There are four lookout levels for visitors. At 1,465 ft, Sky Pod, my observation deck, is the world's highest.

I am the tallest tower in the world at 1,815 ft. There is some controversy about this fact, though much of my height comes from my antennae. I have three legs and a central hollow core to ensure flexibility in winds. Reinforced concrete and post-tensioned steel had been used for this. I am on the north shore of Lake Ontario. It took 40 months to complete my construction.

Canadian National or CN Tower, Toronto, Canada

Since 1997, TrizecHahn Corporation has been managing and operating the CN tower and its adjoining base lands. Under its management, the tower saw a $26 million entertainment expansion and revitalisation from 26 June 1998. The architects of the tower are John Andrews and Webb Zerafa, and Menkes Housden, Toronto (E. R. Baldwin). The tower has 181 storeys.

I am also called Vindhyagiri or Perkalbappu and rise to 3,347 ft above sea level. A flight of 614 steps leads to my summit. The Mauryan Emperor, Chandragupta Maurya can be said to have established me when he handed over his empire to his son Bimbisara and sought my serenity. His only companion then was his Jain guru, Bhagavan Bhadarabahu Swami. Emperor Chandragupta became a Jain ascetic and is said to have ended his days by ritual starvation.

I am situated between two rocky hills, Indragiri and Chandragiri. My site has 37 temples and 525 inscriptions in different languages. My name means the 'monk of the white pond'. Among Jain *bastis* or temples and *maths* or monasteries is the Chandragupta *basti* built by Emperor Asoka, the grandson of Chandragupta Maurya. It has eight carved idols studded with semi-precious stones.

I enjoy the Mahamastakabhisheka festival once every 12 years. This festival attracts devotees from all over the world. Potfuls of honey, almonds, saffron, sandalwood, coconut milk, dates, bananas, poppy seed, *ghee* and even gold and silver coins are poured over the statue of Bahubali.

I have a monolithic statue of Lord Gomateshwara, a Jain saint. The statue is 17 m tall and is the tallest monolithic statue in the world. The sculptor Arstameni was commissioned by the Ganga king, Rachamalla, to build it in AD 981. The statue is situated in the Manjunath temple. Priests climb up to pour coconut milk, turmeric paste and vermillion powder (*sindur*) over the statue. I am the most revered Jain pilgrimage site.

Sravanabelagola, Karnataka, India

Thousands of pilgrims flock to see the magnificent and gigantic statue of Lord Gomateshwara or Bahubali. It is said that Lord Gomateshwara accepted defeat during a war with his brother because he realised how useless these wars were. He renounced the world. Sri Gomatheswar was the son of the first Tirthankara, Adinatha.

The feet of the Bahubali statue. Standing near his toes, a average man would reach a little above the ankles.

I can be said to be a treasure-house of exquisite carvings and works of art from all over the world. My intricately carved doors tell you that my interiors would be similar or even more gorgeous. They are right. You open these doors and step into extremely luxuriously decorated rooms. It is said that I have the largest collection of gold items, quantitywise. My Durbar Hall has an ornate ceiling and many sculptured pillars that I think are painted with gold.

You will find early 19th and 20th-century dolls to the north of my gates, and a ceremonial wooden elephant *howdah* decorated with 84 kg of 24-carat gold. The walls that lead to the Kalyan *mandapa* or the royal wedding hall are lined with elaborate oil paintings, illustrating the Dussehra festival of 1930. The hall has chandeliers and stained glass in peacock designs.

I am a palace built in Indo-Saracenic style with domes, turrets, arches and colonnades. I was originally the residence of the Wodeyar kings. Henry Irwin, the British consultant-architect of Madras state, designed me and I was built in 1912 for the 24th Raja Wodeyar. An earlier wooden palace of the Raja was destroyed by fire in 1897 and the same site was used to build me. Twelve palaces, some of which are from earlier periods, surround me.

I have been converted into a museum to showcase the treasures, souvenirs, paintings, royal costumes, etc. On Sunday evenings and festivals, I am completely lit up by 50,000 light bulbs. To enter me, you have to come through the *Gombe Thotti* or Doll's Pavilion, a gallery of Indian and European objects. If you want to get to my centre, the Elephant Gate is the main entrance you will have to come through. This gate bears the state's royal symbol of a double-headed eagle.

Mysore Palace in Mysore, Karnataka, India

The walls are painted with pictures of the Dussehra processions in such a way that from any angle you can see the procession coming towards you. Krishnamacharya taught yoga at Mysore Palace from the early 1930s until 1950.

I am a Benedictine monastery close to the palace of Edward the Confessor, the last of the Anglo-Saxon kings, who wanted to renovate and enlarge me. I was consecrated on 28 December 1065, and he died a few days later. His mortal remains were entombed behind my high altar. Among the most famous ceremonies that I have witnessed were the coronation of William the Conqueror on Christmas Day, 1066, and the **canonisation** of Edward the Confessor in 1161.

In the middle of the 13th century, Henry III decided to pull me down and rebuild me in a new architectural design. He sent his architect Henry de Reyns abroad to study contemporary developments in architecture. I no longer remained a **Norman Abbey**. They turned me into an architectural masterpiece of the 13th-16th centuries. Today I still have regular worship inside me and am a witness to many royal and great celebrations and events.

I am neither a **cathedral** nor a **parish church**. I have been proclaimed a 'Royal Peculiar', not subject to the rule of any Bishop. I have my own constitution in a charter granted in 1560. Queen Elizabeth I refounded me as a Collegiate Church. Thus, I was given a new shape and outlook to handle the new modern age. The first St. Margaret's church was built by the monks living with me in the latter part of the 11th century so that local people would leave them undisturbed, while at the same time they would receive religious sermons and **sacraments**.

Every monarch since William the Conqueror with the exception of Edward V and Edward VIII was crowned within me. Henry III was the one who transferred the body of Edward the Confessor to a magnificent tomb behind my high altar. Over three thousand people have been either buried or memorialised by me. Notable among these is the Unknown Warrior, whose grave, close to my west door, has become a place of pilgrimage.

Westminster Abbey on Thorney Island, United Kingdom

In 1965-66, the Abbey celebrated its 900th anniversary, taking as its theme 'one people'. A creative new addition to the Abbey was the glorious Lady Chapel built by Henry VII and designed by Nicholas Hawksmoor. The monastic community is now gone, and replaced by a Dean, minor canons and a large lay staff.

We are a group of temples, mostly built by the Chandela Rajputs during AD 950-1050. Our construction took a little over two centuries. In terms of architecture, we are said to portray the highest form of the north Indian ***Nagara*** style. We were a total of 85 temples originally built, but only 20 of us have survived. Most of us who survived, though, are still in excellent condition.

The most popular temples among us are the ones built by the Chandela Rajputs. They were headed by a valiant warrior who fought lions bare-handed. To commemorate this, you can see a warrior fighting with a lion as an emblem on most of us. T. S. Burt, a British engineer, discovered us in the 19th century. General Alexander Cunningham did considerable research on us as a part of his Survey of India reports.

We are mostly known for the large number of sculptures that decorate both our exteriors as well as interiors. There are depictions of gods, celestial beauties or *apsaras*, queens and other female forms in sexual poses. Everywhere you look, walls, windows, pillars, ceilings, they are all carved with these figures. Some of them may be a part of legends and myths, others just depict the imagination and feelings of the people who built us.

We got our name from the date-palm. Until the mid-1960s, no one cared to visit us much, but today we are our country's biggest attraction after the Taj Mahal. Every spring, there is a prestigious seven-day dance festival, where we are the focal point. Our existence is celebrated with passion and joy. This cultural festival highlights Indian classical dance and music, which are believed to have originated in the Hindu temples.

Khajuraho temples, Madhya Pradesh, India

While some temples depict **Shaivism**, a form of Hinduism that concentrates on Shiva, others clearly show the influence of **Vaishnavism**, Jainism, and **tantrism**. Though none of the temples are very large, all of them are awesome with imposing structures because of their elegance and rich surface sculpture. On one temple alone, the figures depicted are over 650 in number.

I am a burial site on a plateau. I am high and flat, overlooking everything. My exact size may never be known. Excavations that take place here find new tombs and artifacts even today. Excavations started in the early 1800s. Any monument placed here can be seen from far away. I also have a ready supply of limestone that makes it easy for people to build.

I have been explored and excavated more thoroughly than any other site in the world. However, people still find new things everyday. I heard Napoleon Bonaparte say to his soldiers before his battle here in 1798: "From atop these pyramids, 40 centuries look down upon you." I am visited by people who want to have a look at the three great pyramids. It is now thought that the three large pyramids of this site are actually meant to be in an alignment resembling that of the three 'belt' stars in the constellation Orion: Alnitak, Alnilam, and Mintaka.

I also have the Sphinx, 'pyramid of the queens', attendant temples and out-buildings, and the private *mastabas* of the nobility. The features of the Sphinx are thought to be those of King Khafre. The *uraeus* (cobra) which originally sat on the king's forehead is now lost, but fragments of his beard are in the Cairo Museum. I have tombs of the first and second dynasty Pharaohs. But it is the tomb of the fourth dynasty Pharaoh, Cheops, which can be said to be the main attraction.

Besides the pyramid of Cheops or Khufu, there is the pyramid of his son, Khephren. Further along the southwest diagonal is the smallest of the three, the pyramid of Khephren's son, Menkaure. The smallest is also the most unusual. First of all, it is not entirely of limestone. The uppermost portions are brick. One theory is that Menkaure died before his pyramid could be completed and the remaining construction was hastily done to finish it in time for the burial.

The Plateau of Giza, Egypt

From the 5th century BC until recently, stones from the monuments were taken and used to build buildings in nearby Cairo. It is believed that had the pyramids not been vandalised, they would still remain to this day much as they were when they were built. There is an Arab proverb that says: 'Man fears times, yet time fears the pyramids.'

I am an impressive building. I was earlier a temple designed by Agrippa in 27 BC. Emperor Hadrian rebuilt me in my present form in AD 117-125. My original rectangular form with 16 granite columns became the porch of my present domed structure. I have an opening at the centre of my dome, which is 8.9 m in diameter. This opening is not covered and when it rains, the water falls on the floor. Due to this, my floor is slightly concave with a drain at the centre.

I was originally a temple dedicated to all Roman gods and later consecrated as a Catholic church. My porch originally faced a courtyard and is now in front of the Piazza della Rotonda. When you open my huge bronze doors, you enter a great circular room, exactly like a cylinder. The walls are 6.05 m thick and hold up my dome. On the lower level of the cylinder are seven niches and a pair of Corinthian columns. Opposite my main door is a semi-circular recess, and on each side are three additional recesses, alternately rectangular and semicircular.

The only natural light that enters me is through the opening at the centre of my dome and through my bronze doors. As the sun moves, light through the skylight creates striking patterns across my walls and floors, which are made of **porphyry**, granite and yellow marbles. My second level was redesigned in 1747 with a row of blind windows alternating with square designs. A part was restored to my original design with six columns and two niches.

My dome has a span of 43.2 m. I was said to have the largest dome until **Brunelleschi's** dome at the Florence Cathedral was built. A whole sphere can be built in my interior. My dome is constructed of stepped rings of solid concrete with decreasing density as lighter and lighter pumice is used, diminishing in thickness to about 1.2 m at the edge of the opening on top.

Pantheon, Rome, Italy

Hidden voids and the interior recesses hollow out this construction, so that it is less a solid mass and more like three continuous **arcades** which correspond to the three tiers of relieving arches visible on the building exterior. The original temple was dedicated to the patron gods of the **Julio-Claudian family**—Venus, Mars and Julius.

I am a city surrounded on all sides by hills. I have forts and am enclosed by walls. A young Bengali engineer and scholar, Vidyadhar Bhattacharya, designed me. My wide, straight bazaars, streets, lanes, residences and uniform rows of shops on either sides of main bazaars are arranged in nine rectangular sectors called *chaukris*. I am the only planned city of my time. I was founded in AD 1727 by one of the greatest rulers of the Kachhawah clan.

I have a number of palaces in and around me. Ajmer palace is a magnificent fort believed to have been the capital of the Minas, the original inhabitants of Rajasthan. Jai Garh is built on a peak and looks over me and the city of Amber. Jal Mahal is a lake-palace surrounded with water. The Government Central Museum is my oldest museum. Designed by Colonel Sir Swinton Jacob, it is located in the centre of the sprawling Ram Niwas Bagh, built in AD 1876, when King Edward VII visited India as the Prince of Wales. It was opened to public in 1886.

I love the Hawa Mahal, one of the buildings that I have. It is a multi-layered palace, with a profusion of windows and stone screens for queens and ladies to see through. One of my main monuments is the Jantar Mantar, which is an astronomical observatory. Johari Bazaar, Tripoliya Bazaar, Chandpole Bazaar, Bari Chaupar, Ajmeri Gate, Sanganeri Gate, Bapu Bazaar, and their lanes like Khazane Walon Ka Rasta, Maniharon Ka Rasta, Gopal ji Ka Rasta, Ghee Walon Ka Rasta, Haldiyon Ka Rasta are some of my main areas.

I was founded by Maharaja Jai Singh II. To create the impression of red sandstone buildings of Mughal cities, I was painted pink. I was painted my present pink colour by Maharaja Man Singh II as a special treat when Prince of Wales, later Edward VII, visited me in 1876. Today, every home and shop that I have is obliged by law to maintain its exterior in the same colour. I am a major gem and jewellery centre, famous for *kundan* and silver work.

Jaipur, Rajasthan, India

Jaipur's lacquer bangles are famous all over the world. There are woollen carpets, cotton rugs, marble statues, enamelled wares, brassware, hand-block printed **Sanganeri** and **Bagru** cotton fabrics, exotic blue pottery made from crushed quartz, leather footwear and much more.

Hawa Mahal

I am a bridge that can be said to be the lifeline of the place I belong to. The area in which I am built has winds blowing at 60 miles per hour and strong ocean currents sweeping through a rugged canyon below my surface — as a result the engineering challenge was enormous. Also, my construction started in the middle of the Great Depression and funds were scarce; further, another bridge, the Bay Bridge was already under construction. My birth was thus not very welcome.

In spite of everything, engineer and bridge-builder, Joseph Strauss persisted, and voters overwhelmingly approved $35 million in bonds to construct me. Construction began in 1933 and was completed in 1937. Strauss was a pioneer in building safety, with innovations including hard hats and daily sobriety tests. While I was being built, only 12 lives were lost; this was an accomplishment considering that in that era, one man was killed on most construction projects for every million spent.

For many years before I was built, the only way to get across my bay was by ferry, and by the early 20th century, the bay was clogged with ferries. Keeping my size in mind, consulting architect Irving F. Morrow felt that I should not have the same intensity of light on all of my parts. The towers were to have less light at the top and as he did not want flashy lights, he chose low-pressure sodium vapour lamps with a subtle amber glow for the roadway.

I am the symbol of the city. I am the subject of many photographs, the result of one man's vision and persistence, and span the entrance to my city's bay. Vikram Seth has written a novel in verse named after me to depict the life in my city. Every autumn, thousands of migrating **raptors** appear over me. I am connected to a National Recreation Area that is one of the largest urban National Parks in the world.

Golden Gate, San Francisco, USA

The Golden Gate Strait is the entrance to the San Francisco Bay from the Pacific Ocean. The Strait is approximately three miles long and one mile wide. It is said that John C. Fremont, captain, Topographical Engineers of the US Army named it 'Chrysoplae' or Golden Gate as it reminded him of a harbour in Istanbul named 'Chrysoceras' or Golden Horn.

Between first century BC and first century AD, I was the centre for arts in the northern part of my country. The style of sculpture and stone-carving styles of this period are named after me. The main theme of these sculptures was inspired by the life of Lord Buddha. By the 5th century BC, I was a major metropolis and the capital of the Surasena kingdom — one of the 16 ***mahajanapadas*** of the period. I now became the eastern capital of the Kushan Emperor Kaniska. My 'golden age' was during the rule of the Kushanas.

I continued as a centre of power up to the Gupta era in the 4th century AD. I am a part of the great northern plains and am situated on the west bank of River Yamuna. I am 145 km south of Delhi and 58 km northwest of Agra. The Jamma Masjid was built inside me by Nabir Khan in AD 1661. The mosque has four minarets with bright coloured plaster mosaic. The Dwarkadheesh temple is my main temple and was built in 1814. Situated on my outskirts, the temple carvings and paintings are a major attraction.

My origins date back to ancient times and I am mentioned in the ancient Indian epic of *Mahabharata*. I was also a part of the Mauryan Empire. King Ashoka, the great Mauryan ruler, built a number of Buddhist monuments in and around me in the 3rd century BC. Nearby is Mansarovar, a wetland grove and bird sanctuary, roughly five acres in size. Birds like heron and the Sarus crane are seen here. The Vishram Ghat on river Yamuna is said to be the place where **Krishna** rested after killing his evil uncle, Kansa.

I am said to be the birthplace of Lord Krishna, the popular incarnation of Lord Vishnu. I, and the areas around me, are linked with the childhood exploits of Lord Krishna. I am an important pilgrim place of the Hindus and one of the seven sacred cities in India. A stone slab marks the original spot of the birth of Krishna. According to legend, Krishna was born in a small prison room. The earlier Kesava Deo temple had the room where Krishna was born.

Mathura in Uttar Pradesh, India

The Archaeological Museum of Mathura or Brajbhoomi has an excellent collection of sculptures belonging to the ancient Mathura school of art. The Dwarkadheesh temple was built in 1815 by Seth Gokuldas Parikh, treasurer of Gwalior state.

The Dwarkadheesh temple in Mathura

Commissioned in 1806 by Napoleon, shortly after his victory at **Austerlitz**, I was completed in 1836. His dream of marching under me in victory was thus cut short by his defeat in Waterloo in 1815. My massive **piers** decorated with **bas reliefs** depict scenes trom the revolutionary era. There are four huge sculptures at the bases of my four pillars. These commemorate The Triumph of 1810; Resistance and Peace; and The Departure of the Volunteers, more commonly known by the name La Marseillaise.

On the day the Battle of Verdun started in 1916, the sword carried by the figure representing the Republic, in the sculpture of La Marseillaise, broke off. The sculpture was immediately hidden to conceal the accident and avoid any undesired interpretations as a bad omen.

Engraved around my top are the names of major victories won during the Revolutionary and Napoleonic periods. The names of less important victories, as well as those of 558 generals, are on my inside walls. Generals whose names are underlined died in action. Beneath my arch is the Tomb of the Unknown Soldier. Here every **Armistice Day** on 11 November, the President lays a wreath. I keep the memory of all the dead killed in the First World War with a permanently burning flame of remembrance.

Napoleon Bonaparte intended me to be a triumphal arch in classical style. I was completed during the reign of Louis Philippe. I am located at the top of the Champs Elysees and the centre of the **Place de L'Etoile**. However, the rest of the Place de L'Etoile was not finished until 1854. Twelve roads lead out from me. I was designed by architect J.F. Chalgrin, who based it on the Arch of Titus in Rome. I am 164 ft high, slightly more than 147 ft wide, and 72 ft deep.

Arch de Triumphe, Paris, France

Inside the Arch there is a small museum documenting its history and construction. From the roof of the Arch we get a spectacular view of Paris. Since it was built, it had never been reworked on until 2003, when work began on renovating it. The estimated cost of this renovation was 2.1 million francs. It was built at a cost of 9.3 million francs.

I am an elliptical stadium. On entering me, visitors had to climb sloping ramps to their seats, according to gender and social class. Women and the poor sat on wooden benches in the fourth tier. If the weather wasn't good or too sunny, an enormous coloured cloth canopy or velarium could be stretched overhead. It took 10 years to build me and when I was complete, I was the largest structure of my type. I was 160 ft high with four storeys.

As many as 50,000 spectators with numbered tickets entered through 76 of my 80 entrances on the ground level to see a match or a show. Two of the remaining gates were kept for the Emperor, and the last two gates were for the participants. My exterior was made of limestone, brick and concrete and topped with marble. My opening ceremony in AD 80 was unlike any other and games and ceremonies went on for 100 days.

Each of my three upper floors consisted of 80 arches. A wooden flooring was used to cover my underground chambers, where the **gladiators** as well as the animals were kept before their performance. During my first 10 years, I was filled with water and I had great fun witnessing mock naval battles. However, the water was damaging to the foundation as well as to the flooring and this practice was stopped.

Most of my shows lasted all day. There were comic and exotic animal shows in the morning and professional gladiator events in the afternoon. In most tournaments and games, it was a fight to death. I saw, oh so many, professional gladiators, who were generally condemned criminals, prisoners of war and slaves, fight either animals or each other, generally until death. Their weapons included nets, swords, tridents, spears, or firebrands. Occasionally, free Romans would enter the fight too for adventure and of course, the glory.

Colosseum, Rome, Italy

Eventually, gladiator fights were outlawed by Emperor Honorius in AD 404; however, animal combats continued for another century. There is no documentation to back up the story of Christians being fed to the lions. After the Roman times, the Colosseum became a fortress, then a source of building materials, a scenery for painters and a place of Christian worship. Today it is used as an **amphitheatre**.

I am a temple built in stone. Only two subsidiary temples out of the 22 that were inside my precincts exist today. I was constructed by Narasinha Deva of Ganga dynasty in mid 13th century. I also have an archaeological museum that you can visit. The Vaishnadevi Mayadevi temple stands to my west. I am in partial ruins.

My roof is covered with sculptures of beautiful heavenly girls. I was also called the 'Black Pagoda' by ancient travellers. I am a World Heritage Site. I do not have a dome or tower over my main shrine. It is said it was not constructed because the foundation was not strong enough to bear the weight. It is also believed that it was constructed but the magnetic dome caused ships to crash near the seashore, and thus was removed.

My main tower stood as high as 227 ft. My *jagmohana* (porch) and I, both stand on top of the stone platform supporting 24 wheels. The intricate carvings on the walls and wheels of the chariot depict the life of those times: royal, social, religious and military. The fine sculptures depicting court life, hunting scenes, celestial deities are epitomes of precision and grace. Sculptures from the *Kamasutra* also adorn me.

I have a collossal image of the chariot of the sun, drawn by seven horses and 24 wheels symbolising the divisions of time. Two lions guard my entrance, while they are crushing elephants. My *natya mandir* or the Dance Hall probably remains as the last remnant of the glorious temples of my state. I have three images of the sun god that catch the rays of the sun at dawn, noon and sunset.

Sun temple, Konark, Orissa, India

Konark is also known as Konaditya. The name Konark is derived from the words: *kona* - corner and *arka* - sun. Konark is also known as *Arkakshetra* or the land of the sun.

One of the wheels of the Sun Temple

I have an area of approximately 40 sq km. There are no motor vehicles inside me and walking and cycling are the two ways you can get around. Walking along raised embankments offers a unique opportunity to get closer to the rich birdlife. If you take a cycle rickshaw, the rickshaw-puller will act as both guide and local bird expert. Boats and horse-drawn *tongas* are also available at times.

I owe my origin to a famous Marharaja, Suraj Mal. He modified my main lake using a system of dykes and sluice gates to produce an artificial swamp. The resultant habitat provided ideal feeding ground for a huge numbers of birds. His intention, however, was to have a good *shikar* later. Whatever the case may be, today of course hunting is not allowed, and in fact there are fights because even the local people who bring in their cattle for grazing, are barred.

Wildlife include rock pythons and various lizards. Resident mammals include *nilgai, chital, sambar*, wild boar, jackal and mongoose. There are also several species of lesser cat though these are rarely seen. I have a stunning variety of indigenous bird life. I am one of the most important breeding and feeding grounds for migratory birds in the world.

Every winter, my bird population swells by three times as birds from as far away as Europe and Siberia visit me. These include the rare Siberian crane. They tell me that they travel half the globe to reach me in the winter. Most of the migratory birds arrive during October and stay until the end of February. During these months, I become an ornithologist's paradise. I was given National Park status in 1982 and became a World Heritage Site in 1985.

Bharatpur or Keladeo Ghana Bird Sanctuary, Rajasthan, India

During the monsoon season, vast colonies of resident birds go into breeding and feeding on the rich aquatic harvest. The Keoladeo Sanctuary has six different species of herons and egrets. Alongside the herons can be seen the painted storks, **ibises, spoonbills, cormorants, paddybirds** and many more species.

I am known as a museum today. In 1546, it was decided that I would be transformed from a fortress into a luxury palace. Pierre Lescot supervised my construction, which continued under Henri II and Charles IX. The construction involved two new wings which occupy two sides of the former fortress. Jean Goujon decorated the exterior and the great hall of this wing. My architecture bears witness to more than 800 years of history.

Established in 1793 as a museum, I am one of the earliest European museums. Divided into seven departments, my collections incorporate works dating from the birth of the great antique civilisations right up to the first half of the 19th century. I became a museum actually as a part of an earlier project, which intended to devote the entire palace to the function of a museum. I cover an area of some 40 hectares right in the heart of the city. I have almost 60,000 m² of exhibition rooms with items representing 11 millennia of culture.

I hope that I reflect all the artistic cultures of Europe. My origin goes back to the *'Cabinet des tableaux'* constituted at Fontainebleau at the beginning of the 16th century. At the end of Louis XIV's reign, I had 1,478 paintings by the masters, making my collection one of the richest European collections of the time. Today I have more than 6, 000 European paintings dating from the end of the 18th century to the mid 19th century, from miniatures to monumental canvases.

The most famous paintings in my collection are *Mona Lisa*, also known as La Gioconda by Leonardo da Vinci; *The Virgin and Child with St. John the Baptist*, known as *La Belle Jardinière* by Raphaël; *The Sermon of St. Stephen at Jerusalem* by Vittore Carpaccio. Besides paintings, I have Oriental, Egyptian, Islamic, Greek, Estruscan and Roman antiquities: sculptures, prints and drawings, African, Asian and American arts and so on. I can be said to be an encyclopaedia of civilisations of the world.

Louvre, Paris, France

The Grand Louvre is a part of the 'Grand Travaux' or Major Works defined by the former President of the Republic, François Mitterrand, which also includes the new Bibliothèque Nationale de France, the Opéra Bastille and the Grande Arche de la Défense.

I am a lake considered to be the most beautiful in my country. I am very shallow and have a heavy growth of waterweeds. This is probably why there are so few powered boats on the water. As you move along, you will often see weeds being pulled up from me. This serves a double purpose: my waterways are kept clear and the weeds, which are rotted, form excellent compost for the gardens.

My floating gardens, known as *Rad*, are one of my fascinating aspects. They're composed of matted vegetation and earth, which are cut away from the lake bottom and towed to a convenient location where they are moored. Vegetables like tomato and cucumber grow amazingly well in these gardens. My recorded existence dates back to 250 BC. I look most beautiful when the lotus flowers bloom in July and August.

The main causeway across me carries the water pipeline for the city's main water supply. A gate at the city end controls my flow into the Jhelum river canal. It's the steady flow of water through me, combined with the relatively cold temperature, which keeps me so clear looking. I will tell you a secret: I am not really one lake at all, but three. More than 100,000 people live on me and I am one of the largest living water bodies in the world.

I am a maze of intricate waterways and channels, floating islands of vegetation, houseboats. The Mughal Gardens can be seen near me. I am slowly but gradually shrinking. About 30 years back, I was 74 sq km in area and today, I am only 13 sq km. This is mainly because the water bodies that make me up are constantly being converted into land mass for growing vegetables and for construction of concrete houses.

Dal Lake, Srinagar, Jammu and Kashmir, India

The lake is divided into Gagribal, Lokut Dal and Bod Dal by a series of causeways. The best way to see it is to take a ***shikara***. The Dal Lake has three islands in it. It's also flanked by hills, particularly along its east bank. The Shankaracharya hill provides a very fine view over the lake. Nagin Lake, which is usually thought of as a separate lake, is also divided from Dal Lake only by a causeway.

I am one of the country's most beautiful cities. There is evidence that I existed and was occupied in prehistoric times but my true foundations are said to be in the Roman times. I originated as one of Caesar's colonies. I was rectangular and was enclosed in a wall about 1800 m long. In the early 12th century, I became a free city and by 1138, I was ruled by 12 consuls, assisted by the Council of One Hundred, a group of rich merchants.

In 1207, due to problems like faction fighting, my council was replaced by a foreign and assumed to be neutral Governor, the *podestà*. The great plague of 1348 cut my population by almost half. I was badly damaged during Second World War by the Germans. Floods ravaged me in the last century, causing great damage to my building and artwork, some of which are still being restored. I am mainly a banking and financial city. However, I do have good engineering, optical, pharmaceutical, chemical, metallurgical, publishing and textile idustries.

The Medicis came to power after the *podestà*, eventually becoming bankers to the **papacy**. The most famous Medici was Lorenzo, who took power in 1469. During his time, art, music and poetry florished. Lorenzo sponsored philosophers and artists such as Botticelli, da Vinci and Michelangelo. I am known for my culinary traditions — my olive oil, meat dishes and of course the famous **chianti**. Some of my beautiful spots include **Ponte Vecchio, Duomo**, the gem-filled **Uffizi Gallery**, the **Piazza della Signoria** and the **Medici Chapels**.

I have a population of 3,51,000. I was founded as a colony of Fiesole in about 200 BC, later becoming the Roman Florentia, a garrison town controlling the Via Flaminia. I was a university town till the time of Charlemagne. I can be said to have given birth to the language of my country by the fact that Dante lived here. According to UNESCO, 60 per cent of the world's most important works of art are located in my country and approximately half of these are with me.

Florence, Tuscany, Italy

The Chianti area, between Florence and Siena, is one of the most beautiful countrysides in Italy and a famous wine-production area. The most important cultural events of Florence are Easter, the Feast of St. John and The 'Historic Football in Costume'. During the Italian Renaissance, Florence acquired its palaces and squares, literally turning into a living museum.

I am a building at a site called Bennelong Point, named after the first **aborigine** in my country to speak English, who was born on the site. Until I was born, it was used as a **wharfing** area and had an ugly tram-storage barn. My construction began in March 1959 and proceeded slowly over the next 14 years. I am perhaps the most efficient place in the world. I operate 24 hours a day, every day of the year except on Christmas and Good Friday.

An international competition was organized to find a designer for me. The winner of the competition, announced in January 1957, was the Danish architect Jorn Utzon. It was originally thought that it would take four years to complete me; in actual fact, I wasn't completed until mid 1973. I am located at the circular **quay**. I have an average of 3,000 events each year with up to a total of two million people as audience. In addition, approximately 200,000 people take a guided tour of me each year.

I have nearly 1,000 rooms, including five main auditoria. I also have a reception hall, five rehearsal studios, four restaurants, six theatre bars, extensive foyer and lounge areas, 60 dressing rooms and suites, library, an artists' lounge and canteen known as the Greenroom, administrative offices and extensive plant and machinery areas. An appeal fund raised money about $900,000 for my construction and the rest of $102 million that was required came from the profits of lotteries released under my name.

I am the busiest performing arts centre in the world. Since my opening in 1973, I have seen hours of entertainment and I attract the best in world-class talent year after year. I saw my first performance in the Opera Theatre on 28 September 1973, a production of War and Peace by Prokofiev. I was officially opened by Queen Elizabeth II on 20 October 1973.

Sydney Opera House, Sydney, Australia

The original design called for two theatres. The government changed its mind and that required the building to be altered and four theatres were incorporated into the design. Recently, there were some internal changes to the structure and a fifth theatre was built.

I cover an area of 430 sq km. I have River Brahmaputra on the north and the Karbi-Anglong hills on my south. National Highway 37 passes through me and the neighbouring tea estates. My animals sometimes wander out to the highway. I was originally established as a reserved forest in 1908. I became a game sanctuary in 1916 and a wildlife sanctuary in 1950. In December 1985, I was designated as a World Heritage Site.

My main problem has always been poaching. In the past few years, my guards have been better equipped and are able to protect me better. I have a large population of wild elephants, Indian bison, swamp deer, hog deer, **sloth bears**, tigers, leopard cats, jungle cats, otters, **hog badgers**, capped langurs, **hoolock gibbons**, wild boar, jackal, wild buffalo, pythons, monitor lizards and the one-horned rhino. I am a birder's paradise. The crested serpent eagle is common while Palla's fishing eagle and grey-headed fishing eagle are frequently seen.

I have three main ranges. Tigers can be regularly sighted in my central range. I have some great perches on this trail for raptor sightings, as well as lakes with otters and groups of wild elephants. My largest lake is in the eastern range and during winter, I see thousands of migratory birds. Rhinos, elephants and buffalo also cool off here. My western range is the best place to see birds, especially raptors. Tigers are also seen on this route, but not as regularly as in the central range.

The main purpose of my existence can be said to be the protection and conservation of the surviving population of the one-horned Indian rhinoceros. You can say that I am a huge success story. My rhino population has increased from 12 according to an estimate at the beginning of the 20th century to over 1,000 now. I see tourists from all over. Since the closing of Manas National Park due to political turmoil, I have become the most important park in the region.

Kaziranga National Park, Assam, India

The park is open from November to April. Elephant safaris take you through the tall elephant grass. Jeep safaris cover a much larger area of the park. Water-birds include swamp partridge, bar-headed goose, whistling teal, florican, storks, herons and even pelicans. A wide variety of snakes and other reptiles including the rock python and the monitor lizard are also seen.

Mahouts waiting to take you around

I have been a famous city since the classical era and have been praised by historians and poets alike, for my beauty and civilisation. I became a Roman colony and after that, got lost, counting the number of gymnasium, porticos, aqueducts, schools, streets, tunnels being built. I was the most popular holiday resort of the Roman fathers, who built their villas along my coastline.

When the last Emperor died, I was conquered. I was made an intellectual capital by Frederic II who founded a university in me. In 1266, with Carlo d'Angiò, I got back my lost glory and became the capital of the kingdom. It was during the time of Robert the Wise that I really got a rebirth. My population increased, buildings increased in number and several colonies of Florentines, Lombards, Catalans and Provençals, established themselves in me. Fresh blood of industries, trade and commerce ran through my veins.

All was not pleasant for me even after this. I saw two centuries of slavery, but somehow I never gave up and continued to grow, especially during Viceroy Pietro de Toledo's government. In 1734, with the Bourbon dynasty coming in, I again became the capital. I owe my grandeur, building development and the construction of monumental works to Charles of the Bourbons. I again became the preferred vacation place for travellers.

I was born in the 6th century BC from the union of two ancient cities of Greek origin, Palepolis and Neapolis. I expanded during the Roman period, and kept my character of a Greek city intact for centuries. The building expansion continued in the 20th century. My new buildings include the Galleria Laziale.

Naples, Italy

During the Second World War, the monuments of Naples suffered very serious damage. Serious renovation and new constructions were made to preserve the culture of this grand coastal city. Across the wide bay is the romantic Isle of Capri, where you can be among the rich and the famous. Nearby is Pompeii destroyed by Mt. Vesuvius in AD 79.

I stand on top of the Hunchback mountain and am 2,310 ft high. I was made by French sculptor Paul Maximilian Landowski. I was inaugurated in 1931 and weigh 1,145 tonnes. Originally, I had been conceived as the national monument in memory of the 100th anniversary of independence of my country from Portugal.

My mountain lies in the middle of Tijuca National Park. Tijuca is the green lung of my city. You can visit me by a special train, called the 'cog train', through the Tijuca. I am located only 15 minutes from the beach of my city, which is also very famous. I am one of the modern wonders of the world. My base has a series of concrete platforms at different heights, finally ending at my feet.

My design was sketched by architect Costa Silva in 1921. I originally had folded arms, and only at the draft stage it was decided to keep my arms outstretched. My lighting arrangements were coordinated by Marconi, the inventor of the radio, from Italy. Though I am made of concrete, I am covered with a **steatite** layer. In my 8 m high base, there is a chapel that can accommodate 150 people.

My mountain is called *Corcovado* in the local language. I have outstretched arms that span 92 ft. I am a replication of Christ and when you look at me, you will feel I am embracing the entire city in my arms. My city had been described by Darwin as "more magnificent than anything any European has ever seen in his country of origin". It was the capital of my country till 1960s. It still remains the carnival capital of the world and 'fun capital' suits it better than any other name.

The Statue of Cristo Redentor, Rio de Janeiro, Brazil

Brazil has some of the best jewels in the world, and the top jewellery store here is H. Stern, the headquarters of which is in Rio. Hans Stern, originally a German immigrant, now owns 180 stores in 40 countries. In Rio, he has a jewellery museum, where the entire process from mining of stones to making of jewellery can be seen.

The statue of Christo Redentor

I am a statue designed by sculptor Frederic Auguste Bartholdi. He was commissioned to complete me in time to commemorate the centennial of the Declaration of Independence of the country where I live. My birth was a joint effort between two nations and it was agreed upon that my pedestal would be built in the place I stay and my main body would be built by the other country.

The financing for my pedestal was completed in August 1885 and its construction was over in April 1886. I was completed in July 1884 and arrived in my new country on board the *'Isere'* from France. As I had to cross an ocean, I was reduced to 350 individual pieces and packed in 214 crates. Visitors need to climb 354 steps to reach my top and 192 steps in order to reach the top of the pedestal.

I was re-assembled on my new pedestal in four months' time. On 28 October 1886, I was inaugurated and dedicated in front of thousands of spectators. I am a national monument. In 1984, the United Nations designated me as a World Heritage Site. On 5 July 1986, I was re-opened to the public during my centennial, after being extensively renovated. I wear sandals on my feet, each of which are 25 ft long.

President Grover Cleveland accepted me on behalf of his country and said: "We will not forget that Liberty has made her home here; nor shall her chosen altar be neglected." The tablet, which I hold in my left hand, reads 'July 4th, 1776.' Many people believe that the sculptor's mother, Charlotte Bartholdi, was the model for me. Other feel I am based on his earlier plans for a statue of the Roman goddess, Libertas, twice the size of the Sphinx, that he wanted to build at the entrance of the Suez Canal.

Statue of Liberty, New York, USA

There are 25 windows in the crown, which symbolise gemstones found on the earth. The seven rays of the statue's crown represent the seven seas and continents of the world. Winds of 50 miles per hour cause the statue to sway 3 ins and the torch sways 5 ins. Bartholdi had to visit USA to 'sell' the idea to the government. On his way back, he wrote: 'Everything in America is big.... Here, even the peas are big.'

I am one of the modern wonders of the world. I represent the first 150 years of my country's independence. I was built between 1927 and 1941 by Gutzon Borglum and 400 workers. I am a part of the Black Hills. Apart from my main structure, I also have a Sculptor's Studio built in 1939 to display unique plaster models and tools related to the sculpting process.

John Gutzon de la Mothe Borglum studied art in many places including San Francisco and Paris. If it was not for him, I would have been a memorial to local heroes. It was his refusal to work on a smaller scale that made me a national monument. He skilfully used dynamite to remove large amounts of rock. His powdermen became so skilled that they could blast to within 4 ins of the finished surface, so much so that 90 per cent of the 450,000 tonnes of granite removed was with dynamite.

The place where I live was inhabited by the **Arikara Indians** from 1500. They were followed by the **Cheyenne, Kiowa, Pawnee** and **Crow**. The **Sioux** came here in the 1700s and 'ruled' over the land for more than 150 years. Francois and Joseph La Verendrye claimed the region for France in 1743. The territory was purchased from Napolean by Thomas Jefferson. In December 1923, Doane Robinson, superintendent of the State Historical Society visualised a massive mountain memorial carved from stone.

The four faces on me depict my country's journey from birth to becoming a super power. Washington saw my country's birth. Jefferson had the ability to dream big and expanded my nation. Lincoln gave my country the ideals of equality and freedom and Roosevelt developed the nation into a world power. I represent the fact that the ideals of these four Presidents were as solid as the rock on which their figures are carved.

Mount Rushmore National Memorial, South Dakota, USA

Gutzon created a model of the four Presidents on a model, one inch on which represented a foot on the cliff. This model can be seen at the Sculptor's Studio. Gutzon died when Mount Rushmore was nearing completion and his son, Lincoln, spent another seven months after his father's death bringing the monument to its current state.

I am a monument designed by John Nash. In my centre is a column, which has a 17 ft-high statue on the top. Around the base of the column are four giant bronze lions. Suronding me, you will see the church of St. Martin's in the fields and the National Gallery, which houses one of the world's richest collections of paintings. I am also famous for my pigeons.

I was built in honour of Admiral Nelson. The bronze lions were sculpted by Sir Edwin Landseer, who was known more for his animal paintings then, and cast by Marocchetti. I also have my city's smallest police station. My site originally had the royal mews for hawks and then the royal stables. Before the statue of Nelson was installed, it is said that 14 stone-masons held a dinner on its flat top.

I am a favourite place for demonstrators and marchers trying to gain attention for their cause. The people of Norway gift an enormous Christmas tree to my country each year, which is erected on me. This gesture by Norway is a 'thank you' to my country for its role in liberating their country during the Second World War. Thousands of people gather here to welcome each New Year.

In 1805, French and Spaniards sailed towards my country from Cadiz. A squadron commanded by Admiral Nelson met them off Cape Trafalgar. In the battle that followed, my country was victorious but the Admiral was killed. I am in memory of this victory of 1805. This battle was the beginning of my country's supremacy in the sea.

Trafalgar Square, London, United Kingdom

A statue of Charles I on horseback at the south end of the square is the original site of Charing Cross. This is the spot from which all 'distances from London' are measured. Edward I had erected a cross here in 1290, marking one of the resting place of the funeral **cortege** of his wife as it made its way to Westminster Abbey. The cross was destroyed during the civil war in the mid-17th century.

I am said to be India's first modern attempt at conserving its wildlife in a protected area. I am the third oldest National Park in the world, born in 1936. My original name was Hailey National Park. Initially only 325 sq km of my magnificent sal forests were protected. In 1952 I was rechristened Ramganga National Park and in 1957, I got my present name.

I am divided into three distinct geographical areas — the Kumaon Himalaya, **Bhabar** tracts, and the **terai** grasslands famous for the wild herds of elephants. I am a mix of hilly areas of deciduous mixed forests, as well as low-lying ground with ravines and vast dense forests of sal trees. The magnificent Ramganga river flows through me and provides life to my animals and birds. My elevation ranges between 400 m and 1,210 m. The multipurpose hydel dam at Kalagarh lies on my southwestern fringe.

My varied **topography** gives me an abundance of indigenous fauna and flora.There are 110 tree species, 37 species of grass, 50 mammals, 25 reptiles and nearly 600 bird species. I am the only National Park in the country that has the Himalayan black bear, Himalayan **palm civet** and the **ghoral**. I have a large numbers of Indian elephants. The reptiles I find most interesting are: the *gharial* and the fresh water **mugger**. I have four types of deer: *sambar* and spotted deer, and the much rarer **muntjac** and hog deer.

I am named after a legendary hunter and writer who is famous for his escapades with the maneater tigers during 1907 and 1941. I was chosen as one of the Project Tiger reserves in 1970, and by the late eighties I merged with the Sonadi Wildlife Sanctuary. I now became over 1,300 sq km in size. Tigers love me because I have abundant prey species and a dense cover. However, it is not so easy to see the tigers because of the dense habitat. I also have leopards and lesser cats, such as the fishing cat and jungle cat.

Corbett National Park, Uttaranchal, India

It is a part of the Nainital and Pauri Garhwal districts in Uttaranchal state, about 250 km from Delhi. It has a huge number of migratory birds. There are also high-altitude species such as the Lammergeier and Steppe eagle. The park is open from November to June, and safaris are available by jeep and elephants.

Entering the wilds on jeep

I am a church built on the design of Baccio Pontelli by Giovannino de Dolci. I originally served as a **Palatine chapel** and take my name from Pope Sixtus IV, who commissioned me. I am a large rectangle with a barrel-vaulted ceiling and I am divided into two unequal parts by a marble screen. My screen and the **transenna** were built by Mino da Fiesole and other artists. The first **Mass** inside me was celebrated on 9 August 1483.

The frescoes on my long walls illustrate parallel events in the lives of Moses and Christ and were executed between 1481 and 1483 by Perugino, Botticelli, Cosimo Rosselli and Domenico Ghirlandaio, with their assistants. My two fresco cycles underline the continuity between the **Old Covenant** and the New Covenant, or the transition from the **Mosaic law** to the Christian religion.

I am one of the most famous chapels in the world. The conclave for the election of the Pope, and other solemn pontifical ceremonies, are held inside me. I measure 40.93 m by 13.41 m, the exact dimensions of the temple of Solomon, as given in the Old Testament. I am 20.70 m high and am roofed by a flattened barrel vault, with little side vaults over the centred windows.

My barrel-vaulted ceiling is entirely covered by the famous frescoes painted by Michelangelo between 1508 and 1512 for Pope Julius II Della Rovere.
The original design was only to have represented the apostles. It was modified at the artist's insistence and became an enormously complex iconographic theme, which may be seen as the representation of mankind waiting for the coming of God.

Sistine Chapel, Vatican City

More than 20 years later after the ceiling was completed, Michelangelo was summoned back by Pope Paul III Farnese to paint the Last Judgment on the wall behind the altar. He worked on it from 1536 to 1541. The chapel was restored recently and its restoraton inauguration ceremony took place on 11 December 1999.

I am perhaps one of the most dazzling monuments of the world. Though I am holy in my entirety and people come to me in thousands to offer prayers, there are nine places within me which are considered to be the holiest. These are the Buddha image with the ruby eye, the wizard Buddha, the Shin Saw Pu Buddha, the Dhammpala Buddha, the Hair Relic Spring, the BoBoAung-Gu Buddha, the Shin Mahtee Buddha, the Upturned Palm Buddha, the Vibrant Mercury Buddha.

I have a complex geometrical shape. Around me are many smaller shrines for pre-Buddhist gods called Nats, which can do miracles. There is even a wish-granting stone. In front of the 72 shrines surrounding me, there are images of lions, serpents, ogres, yogis, spirits, or *wathundari* (an angel). There are four tunnels leading into my base. No one is sure, not even me, of what is inside. According to some, there are flying and turning swords that never stop. I believe them.

I am said to be more than 2,500-years old. My most significant feature is the eight genuine *sandaw* (hair of head) of Gautam Buddha kept as treasures with tremendous amount of precious stones and other jewellery inside me. I am on top of Thein Gottara Hill, the highest in the city. I am made up of 10 parts: the Diamond Bud, the Vane, the Crown, the Plantain Bud-Shaped Bulbous Spire, the Ornamental Lotus Flower, the Embossed Bands, the Inverted Bowl, the Bell, the Three Terraces, and the Base.

I am a solid brick *stupa* completely covered with gold. My lower part is plated with 8,688 solid gold bars, and the upper with another 13,153. My tip is set with 5,448 diamonds, 2,317 rubies, sapphires, and other gems, and 1,065 golden bells. At the very top, I have a single 76-carat diamond. I have a giant banyan tree inside my walls that was grown from the original banyan where Buddha gained enlightenment.

Shwedagon Pagoda, Yongon, Myanmar (Burma)

According to legend, two Burmese merchant-brothers visited the Buddha. They offered him cakes and asked him for a gift. Buddha gave them eight hair which were enshrined in a ruby casket on the Singuttara hill, which was already a shrine. The relic was put in a chamber, over which was built a *stupa* of gold. Over this was built a silver *pagoda*, then a gold and copper, then an iron, then a marble, and then finally a brick *pagoda*, covered with gold.

I am the bell tower of a cathedral. The citizens of my city were very good sailors and conquered many lands, including Jerusalem, Carthago, Ibiza, Mallorca, Africa, Belgium, Britania, Norway, Spain, and Morocco. But they had only one real enemy, the people from Florence. It is to show that they too were as good as the Florence citizens and could build equally good buildings, I was built, along with the rest of the buildings near me — the Cathedral, Baptistry and cemetery.

My construction began in the August of 1173 and continued for about 200 years. No one seems to know clearly who my architect is. After they started constructing me, the war with Florence started again and construction stopped. In 1180, it was again started and in 1185, my first, second, and the third floors were complete. And again came the war with Florence, which of course, meant that all money needed to be put in warfare. Bells were put on the top of my third floor in 1198. In 1319 they finished all my floors and the bells were put on top in 1350. In 1392, my city was sold to Florence.

A widow, called Berta of Bernardo, living in the Santa Maria Institution, is said to have left in her testment 60 'coins' to the '*Opera Campanilis petrarum Sancte Marie*', to purchase some stones to build me. However, as I said, no one, not even me, knows who actually commissioned me. And did I tell you that Galileo is connected to me as well? It is said that he learnt that the acceleration of all free falling objects is the same by throwing a canon ball and a wooden ball from my top! This may or my not be true...I am not saying anything.

When the construction reached about 1.5 m of the third floor, I leaned fearfully, so this was another reason for the halt in my construction apart from the war. In the past it was widely believed that my inclination was part of the project and I was always intended to incline. This is not true at all. I was designed to stand tall and proud but started inclining on my own. I lean about 1/20 in every year. About 18 ins have been corrected. I leaned by 5.2 m in 1997. Needless to say, I am one of the wonders of the world.

Leaning Tower of Pisa, Florence, Italy

During its construction, efforts were made to halt the incipient inclination through the use of special construction devices; later columns and other damaged parts were substituted more than once. Today, interventions are being carried out within the sub-soil in order to significantly reduce the inclination and to make sure that the tower will have a long life. The Pisa Commission is in charge of saving the dangerously tilted structure. It was closed to public from 1990 to 2001.

I am the birthplace of a 4,500-year-old civilisation. Nearly 4,000 specimens of a script carved on stone, pottery and other objects has been discovered in me. However, they have not been deciphered satisfactorily. I was discovered in 1922, and was once an important city. My civilisation was extremely meticulous and had standards for eveything. In fact, same sized bricks and standard weights were used for a thousand miles.

R.D. Banerji was the first to excavate my site and reveal me to the modern world. Archaeologists since then have uncovered streets and brick houses, a covered drainage system and a public bath-house. Many findings, including intriguing necklaces, are displayed in a local museum. There is evidence of trade with Saurashtra and Deccan. Silver and **lapis lazuli** were imported from Persia and Afghanistan, **jadeite** from Tibet and Central Asia.

My civilisation grew up on the banks of River Indus and extended to the Yamuna river along the bed of River Ghaggar in Rajasthan, Gujarat and up to Rivers Narmada and Tapti. The dates of the Indus Valley culture are approximately 2300-2000 BC. Though the Saraswati or the Ghaggar-Hakra river is now dead, its bed is slowly being traced by researchers. Along its flow, a whole new set of ancient towns and cities have been discovered.

My name literally means ‘mound of the dead’. My most striking building is perhaps the great bath, which measures 39 x 23 x 8 ft. It probably had a ritual significance. A few of my seals were found in Mesopotamia, which point towards trade between the two civilisations. Some of the famous figures found inside me are a dancing girl in bronze and a priest draped with a shawl.

Mohenjodaro, South Pakistan

Since 1986, the joint Pakistan-America Harappa Archaeological Research Project has been carrying out the first major excavations at the site in 40 years. These excavations prove that Harappa was far larger than once thought, perhaps supporting a population of 50,000 at certain periods.

I am the highest mountain in my country and one of the largest free-standing mountains in the world. I have three volcanic centres. Early Arab and Chinese traders and historians mention me as a giant mountain but very few early traders tried to come near me to explore me better. I saw many a slave trader passing by me. It was only in the middle of the 19th century that a more serious interest was taken in me.

My area above 8,850 ft comprises a National Park, established in 1973. My park has six **corridors** through the forest reserve by the same name. The forest reserve, which is also a game reserve, was established in 1921. There are five distinct ecological zones from my base to the peak. My lower slopes have coffee and banana fields. Next comes my mountain forests. My tree ferns grow up to 20 ft, and the **giant lobelia** often reaches 30 ft.

At about 9,000 ft, grasslands and shrubbery suddenly appear, and you can also see elephants roaming about. At about 13,000 ft, I become hostile and not much life can be seen except for small mosses and lichens. On my summit, my three glaciers are the only 'moving' things you can expect to meet. At one point, my summit was covered by ice that was more than 100 m deep.

At 5,963 m, I am the highest point in my continent. I lay on a tectonic line intersection. I am technically a volcanic mountain. The activity that created me is less than a million years old. Kibo is my highest volcanic centre and the central ash pit on it is only several hundred-years old. Shira and Mawenzi, my other centres, became inactive before Kibo, which is also the best preserved centre with three concentric craters. The rim of the outer crater of Kibo rises to the 19,340-ft Uhuru Point, which is technically my summit.

Mount Kilimanjaro, Tanzania, Africa

In 1848, Johann Rebmann, a German missionary, saw the mountain and was regaled with tales of adventure by his guide. His tales in turn started to interest people in Germany and several expeditions were organised. The first expedition was by Baron von Decken. On 5 October 1889, Dr Hans Meyer became the first person to finally stand on the summit.

I am a historical monument. Shaheed Udham Singh, one of my country's matryrs, was the survivor of a terrible incident that happened inside my walls. He was 12-years old at that time. Presently I also have a park and a Martyr's Gallery. I am situated just adjacent to an important place of worship for the Sikhs. My Martyr's Gallery is open from 9 a.m. to 5 p.m. in summers and from 10 a.m. to 4 p.m. during winters.

I am situated in the heart of the town. I was more or less an open enclosure with tall buildings on all the four sides with a narrow passage which led into me. I was the property of the family of Sardar Himmat Singh, a noble in the court of Maharaja Ranjit Singh, who originally came from the village of Jalla. The family was collectively known as Jallhevale, although their principal seat later became Alavarpur in Jalandhar district.

Once a garden or garden house, in 1919, I was an uneven and unoccupied walled space, used more as a dumping ground. A plan was announced for turning me into a national memorial during the time when P.V. Narasimha Rao was my country's Prime Minister. A committee was formed under the chairmanship of Narasimha Rao to give a final shape to the plan and its implementation by the Human Resource Development Ministry. There are also plans for expansion of the Martyr's Gallery.

On the morning of 13 April 1919, a peace gathering of 20,000 people took place inside me. Many who had gathered were villagers on a visit to the town on the occasion of the ***Baisakhi*** fair, and were probably unaware of the announcements that asked people not to gather together. General Dyer ordered soldiers to block my entrance and without warning, opened fire. The firing continued for about 20 minutes. 1,650 rounds of .303-inch ammunition were fired. Some people jumped into a well that was there inside me; others just fell down dead.

Jallianwala Bagh in Amritsar, Punjab, India

Dyer's own estimate of the killed was between 200 and 300. The official figures were 379 killed and 1,200 wounded. According to Pandit Madan Mohan Malaviya, who personally collected information with a view to raising the issue in the Central Legislative Council, over 1,000 were killed. The total crowd was estimated at between 15,000 and 20,000,

The memorial at Jallianwala Bagh

I am a famous monument. I am the city's best-known landmark and I look most spectacular at night. When Parliament is in session, a light shines above my front. I have a bell that came originally from the old palace of Westminster. William III gave it to the Dean of St. Paul's. Before returning to Westminster to hang in its present home, it was refashioned in White Chapel in 1858. My bell was cast in White Chapel Bell Foundry, and the first chime rung in situ on 31 May 1859.

On the night of 16 October 1834, Sir Charles Barry, an architect, saw a fire in the old palace and discovered that the houses of Parliament were on fire. Following the destruction of the buildings, a competition was launched for a design suitable for the new palace, in which he put in an entry. Charles Barry's design, in which he had included me, won.

I am essentially a clock tower. The four dials of my clock are 23 sq ft, the minute hand is 14 ft long and the figures are 2 ft high. Minutely regulated with a stack of coins placed on the huge pendulum, it is an excellent timekeeper, which has rarely stopped. During the Second World War, a bomb destroyed the Commons Chamber of the Houses of Parliament, but I remained intact and continued to keep time.

The chimes of my bell were first broadcast on radio on 31 December 1923. There is a microphone in my turret connected to Broadcasting House. I have many attractions nearby, including 10, Downing Street with its famous black front door, which has been the official residence of my country's Prime Ministers since 1732. My bell is named after the first Commissioner of Works, Sir Benjamin Hall.

Clock tower of Big Ben, London, United Kingdom

There are cells within the clock tower where members of Parliament can be imprisoned for a breach of parliamentary privilege, though this is rare. The last recorded case was in 1880. The tower is not open to the general public. The name 'Big Ben' refers not to the clock-tower itself, but to the 13-tonne bell.

I am the world's second highest waterfall. My river is fairly young, only 12,000 years old, but my **escarpment**, which was created by erosion is much older. The glaciers pressed down on the land during the last Ice Age and laid down layers of sediment, as a result of which the slow process of erosion of ice and water ate at the surface of the escarpment.

One-fifth of all the fresh water in the world lies in the four Upper Great Lakes: Michigan, Huron, Superior and Erie. All the outflow empties into the river and eventually cascades over me. After I fall down, the water travels 15 miles over many gorges until it reaches the fifth great lake, Ontario. The land between the lakes does not slope at an even grade, but forms a spectacular drop, approximately the same height as a 20-storey building and this is known as the escarpment. Two billion years ago, this was buried under a blanket of ice.

Man has not been able to completely control the flow of the water over me though even modern engineers have tried. In the past 10 years, two daredevils lost their lives in trying to conquer me. Much of the water today is fed through underground channels and pipes to nearby hydroelectric power stations.

I straddle the international border of my country and attract some 12 million tourists every year. The length of my brink is 2,600 ft, my height is 167 ft and the volume of water that flows over me is 2,271 litres per second. The mighty river plunges over a cliff of **dolostone** and **shale**. On the eastern part of Goat Island, you can find my American Falls, and on the western side, my Horseshoe Falls where the river angles some 90 degrees. My flow was halted over both falls on 30 March 1848 due to an ice jam in the upper river.

Niagara Falls, Canada and United States of America

The word 'Niagara' is derived from the Iroquois Indian word *Onguiaahra* meaning 'the strait'. Approximately 500 years ago, the Niagara river split into two channels, and Goat Island was formed, named after John Stedman, whose goatherds froze to death in the winter of 1780.

I am a lake that attracts a lot of wildlife. Apart from birds, I am visited by black-buck, spotted deer, golden jackals and hyenas. I have around 160 species of fish, crustaceans, and dolphins. More than 0.5 million fisher-folk depend on me for their livelihood. Every morning you will see hundereds of boats sailing into me with fishng nets. Prawn, crab and mackerel fishing is an important 'industry' here.

I am one of the best places in India for bird-watching, and you will see white bellied sea eagles, greyleg geese, purple moorhen, jacana, herons and flamingo. I support one of the world's largest breeding colonies of flamingoes. Nalabana, a forest of reeds famous for winter migratory birds in winter, and Birds Island can be found near me. The Nilgiri Biosphere Reserve near me has India's second largest elephant population. I get nearly 50-70 species of migratory birds each winter.

In 2002, I won the international Ramsar Conservation Award from the Standing Committee of the Ramsar Convention in Switzerland for the work done 'in the field of restoration and wise use of wetlands involving local communities.' I have well-defined sectors of pure seawater, brackish water and fresh water. During the 1971 India-Pakistan war, a refugee camp was set up nearby. The refugees were provided fertilisers for cultivation which leached into me. This led to my **eutrophication**.

I am Asia's largest inland salt-water lagoon. I have many small islands on me, including the Honeymoon Island and Breakfast Island. I am pear-shaped and my waters spread across 1,100 sq km. A basic training institute of the Indian Navy is named after me. A narrow opening in my long barrier spit connects me to the Bay of Bengal. The traditional fishermen around me had to take to the streets to demand the stoppage of large-scale commercial shrimp cultivation that was carried out in me.

Chilka Lake, Puri, Orissa, India

The inlet channel gets choked and very little exchange of material take place between the lagoon and the sea. Chilka was thus faced with a shrinking lagoon cut off from the sea and which was growing less saline. Fish and biodiversity declined. Chilka is a biodiversity hot-spot supporting a number of species listed in the **IUCN** red list.

My name means a fortified town. I was once the hunting lodge of Prince Yuri and was situated on top of a hill overlooking the Moskva and Neglina rivers. Within a century, I became an independent principality within the Mongol Empire. I turned from a modest hunting lodge to an imposing fortress city. I am a self-contained city with palaces, armouries, and churches.

I link my modern nation to its legendary past in the ancient state of Kievan Rus. Some of my important sites are: the Arsenal, Senate, Tsar Cannon and Bell, Cathedral Square, Ivan the Great Belltower, Cathedral of Assumption, Church of the Deposition of the Robe, Cathedral of the Archangel Michael, Cathedral of the Annunciation, Cathedral of the Twelve Apostles, Patriarch's Palace, and the Armoury.

The Czar cannon was built in 1586 and is said to be the largest cannon in the world. It is 16 ft long and weighs 31,725 kg. Master craftsman Andrei Chokov was commissioned for this giant bronze weapon by Czar Fyodor I, Ivan the Terrible's son, for my protection. The Czar's bell was commissioned by Czarina Anna I as a fulfilment of the dream of her grandfather, Czar Alexei. It was to be the biggest and clearest sounding bell in the world but before it was raised, it cracked in a fire in 1737. Today it weighs 200 tonnes but cannot ring.

By the middle of the 14th century, my kingdom was made the seat of my country's Orthodox Church. With Ivan the Great, my kingdom's rule extended over the entire country, and I became more magnificent. Over the next two centuries, I was the central stage for the politics of my rulers till Peter the Great transferred the capital elsewhere. I again became the capital in March 1918. It was as if I got a rebirth. However, I am very much still the majestic city of my old rulers.

The Kremlin, Moscow, Russia

The Grand Kremlin Palace was the new imperial residence, commissioned by Czar Nicholas I in 1838. It was the largest structure in the Kremlin— 500,000 sq ft and cost 11 million rubles to build. It has glorious reception halls, a ceremonial red staircase and private imperial apartments.

I am a lake. On my shore you will find Kisumu, a quiet port town with wide streets and fine colonial architecture. To my south, fishing villages line the lake towards the broad waters of Homa Bay. This area is home to Ruma National Park, a small but attractive park with many unique species. A traditional way of accessing my border is by a cycle-taxi called the *boda boda* (border-border).

neTotal recoverable coal reserves in my region amount to 220 million tonnes. The Sondu Miriu project for building a 60-MW hydroelectric power station along Lake Victoria is constructed by Konoike Construction JV, Vieddeke Heavy Construction Company of Norway, and Murray & Roberts Contractors International of South Africa. Funded largely by the Japan Bank for international cooperation, the project went on hold in June 2001 when funds were suspended due to environmental concerns.

I am 67,493 sq kms in size and am commonly known as Nyanza. I am twice the size of Wales. You will hear the haunting calls of the fish-eagles in trees along my shore. Forty years earlier, the English explorer Speke, travelled along my western shore and reached a place which he named Ripon Falls. This, he said, was the source of one of the greatest rivers in the world.

The Nile flows northwards, carrying my waters to Egypt and beyond into the Mediterranean. I am rich in fish life, with shimmering shoals of colourful cichlids and large Nile perch. My province, Nyanza, is the heartland of the Luo, a tribe known as 'formidable fisherman'. I also give rise to the highest waterfalls in the world.

Lake Victoria, Kenya, Tanzania and Uganda, South Africa

The waters of the lake create the Victoria Falls. The best way to appreciate the beauty of this region is on the lake itself. The sun shines brightly and a gentle breeze rises from the water. Sunsets turn the water to gold, as the local fishermen in their boats pull in their nets and slowly turn towards home.

I am a city that almost all caravan routes passed through during the time of Prophet Muhammad. I have been revered as a holy city from ancient times. I am considered to be the first place created on earth. My main economic activity is provision of services to pilgrims. I have a rugged landscape consisting mostly of solid granite, with rocks sometimes reaching 1,000 ft above sea level. I was ruled by the Ottoman Turks from 1517 until 1916.

I have been first mentioned by the geographer Ptolemy in the 2nd century AD by the name of Macoraba. I was ruled by the Egyptians in the 13th century. In the 16th century Turkey took me over. From 1517, the *sharifs*, or descendants of Muhammad through Hasan, governed me. The Turks were driven away from me in 1916 by Sharif Husein ibn Ali, who later became the first king of Al Hijâz. In 1924, I was occupied by Abdul Aziz ibn Saud, then Sultan of Najd, who made me the religious capital of my country.

I am the most holy city in Islam. I have 1.4 million inhabitants. I am located about 80 km from the Red Sea coast, around a natural well. I am the birthplace of Prophet Muhammad. Non-Muslims are not permitted to enter me. Prophet Muhammad began to preach within me but was forced to flee to Medina. He returned with 10,000 men to conquer and establish me as the centre of the Islamic world. I was ruled by the Carmathians from AD 930 until 1269, when the Egyptian Mamelukes gained control.

I have in my heart the *kaaba*. It is a rectangular building made of bricks. Around the *kaaba* is a great mosque, al-Haram, which can hold 3,00,000 people. Within the precincts of the mosque is the sacred well, called the Zamzam, which was reputedly used by Hagar, mother of Abraham's son, Ishmael. The Quran says: "We have rendered the shrine (the *kaaba*) a focal point for the people and a safe sanctuary. You may use Abraham's shrine as a prayer house."

Mecca, Saudi Arabia

Every year some two million pilgrims attend the Haj. This number is now regulated and each country can send a fixed number of adherents. The numbers of Muslims coming to Mecca for the *Umra* are not regulated. Mecca's older name was Bakkah and the Quran says: "The people owe it to God that they shall observe Haj to this shrine, when they can afford it."

The *kaaba* and al-Haram

I am one of the best-protected sanctuaries in my country with as many as 800 guards. Apart from protecting me, they are also required to fill up my numerous artificial water holes. This is very important in periods of low rainfall as they attract lions who can then also prey on species, which have rapidly increased in number. The feeding habits of the lions have now changed back to a 'normal' pattern with wild ungulates accounting for 70 per cent of their kills.

I am also home to several Negro families called Siddhi. They only marry within their own community and are Muslim. They are landowners in their own right. There seems to be very little information on where they came from originally. Some animals that you can see within me are: four-horned antelope (the only four-horned ungulate in the world), wild boar, wolf, hyena, jackal, jungle cat, *chinkara*, blue bull, marsh muggers as well as a wonderful variety of bird species.

The government has put up legal notices to bar the local pastoral tribe called Maldharis from my interiors. The reason for this is their ongoing conflict with the lions, which again is due to loss of domestic livestock. However, the Maldharis still live here and they are very much a part of me. They still lose some livestock to the lions during the day. They live a nomadic way of life and are strictly vegetarian. Sale of their dairy products is the mainstay of their economy.

I am a success story. From 20 lions in the beginning of the 20th century, I now have 300. In fact I am not big enough to support so many and two smaller populations have been established to the south and north of the park boundaries. I am also home to one of the largest leopard population in India. I am a famous lion sanctuary and am at the bottom of a peninsula with a rugged terrain.

Gir Lion Sanctuary, Gujarat, India

The sanctuary is open from mid October and wildlife viewing is by jeep. A story goes that the Nawab of Junagadh visited Africa at the end of the 18th century and brought back some slaves. This community of pure African origin then settled in Jambur next to the sanctuary and became the Siddhi community of today.

I am a valley situated at the confluence of the streams flowing from Sheshnag Lake and River Lidder. I am also called the 'valley of the shepherds'. I am at a height of 2,130 m and have breathtaking views. Picturesque villages are scattered all over me. *Chinar*, mulberry, poplar, willow trees jostle for space with walnut, apple and pear trees laden with fruits. Sometimes hay is stacked on trees to serve as the winter fodder for animals.

River Lidder is excellent fishing zone for the brown trout. The fishing season stretches from April to September. The word *lidder* is a corruption of *lambodari* which means a 'long-bellied' goddess. The main stream receives a number of tributaries. The houses built on me are generally two storeys high, the ground storey being a cattle-shed. Only a very small window opens from this part of the ground floor which is called *dangij*. The roof is generally covered with rice-grass.

The most beautiful place near me is Baisaran meadow surrounded by thick pine forests. Hajan is an idyllic spot above me. There is a Shiva temple here, generally considered to be my state's oldest existing temple, dating to the 5th century. How do people living in me get water? Simple! A small rill diverted from the main canal enters their compound where they clean their utensils.

I also have beautiful trekking areas. Among pilgrims, the favourite is: Chandanwari - Sheshnag - Panchtarni - Amarnath cave temple - Sonamarg. This is also called the Amarnath *yatra*. Chandanwari, 16 kms from me, is the starting point. About 11 kms from Chandanwari is the mountain lake of Sheshnag (3,574 m). During the month of Sawan, an ice stalagmite forms a natural *Shivalinga* in the Amarnath cave.

Pahalgam, Jammu and Kashmir, India

A famous tourist resort, the climate here is cool even during the height of summer when the maximum temperature does not exceed 25°C. It is set between fairly steep hills. Pahalgam Club has a nine-hole golf course, which can be used by tourists.

I am a place on earth where a very interesting phenomenon is seen. Apart from the effect by the moon, the tides on the earth are influenced by a number of factors like the size and depth of the ocean basin, its inlets, earth's rotation, winds and atmospheric pressure. Between low and high tide, there is normally a range of 1 m or 2. There are some places with almost no difference between the tides and others with extremely great differences between the tides. I belong to the latter category.

I show you vast areas of uncovered sea-bottom during low tide. My 'beach' during the phase between a low and a high tide becomes a very huge, flat plan. I am visited by thousands of migratory shorebirds on their way to South America. They are attracted by the **crustaceans** and worms that surface in my muddy beach. After eating their fill with me, they can then fly for three to four days non-stop. They are best seen within two hours of high tide when thousands line what is known as my 'flats' or 'mud flats'.

My flats are today also rich farmland. Dykes have been built across me for this purpose. In some areas, you can see thousands of acres of fields. It is said that this tradition of farming here began with the Acadian settlers in the 17th century. Durng high tide, the waters of the ocean also push their way up on my rivers against the flow of freshwater coming out. This is called a tidal bore.

I have the honour of having the highest tides on the earth. Minas Basin at one end of me has an average tide range of 12 m, and can reach 16 m. It is at Cape Split in the Minas Basin that this phenomenon should be seen. When a tide is midway, a hollow roar echoes through the forests. The current exceeds 4m/s, and the strength of flow in the deep 5 km-wide channel on Cape Split is equal to the combined flow of all the streams and rivers of the earth. A tide lasts for three hours.

Bay of Fundy, Nova Scotia, Canada

The energy of tides comes from the rotational energy of the earth. Near Annapolis Royal in Nova Scotia, there is the only tidal power plant in the Western Hemisphere, where some of this energy is converted into electrical energy. The peak output is 20 MW, about 1 per cent of Nova Scotia's electrical power capacity.

Boats stranded against the dykes during low tide

I am one of the best preserved and excavated sites of the civilisation I represent. I was occupied from around 200 BC to AD 900 with a peak population of about 60,000-1,00,000. I was discovered in 1848, but excavation and restoration took place only from 1956-1969. I am so much in the interiors, that it is only in the past 10-15 years that visitors have been able to reach me without difficulty. About 3,000 constructions have been discovered and it seems that there are thousands more buried under the thick tropical forest.

I have stunning temples and hundreds of stone buildings and structures like stepped pyramids with underground burial chambers; stone altars for human sacrifice and chiselled stone tablets called *stelae*, which were basically the calender and almanac of my people. I was visited during the 1800s and early 1900s on horseback. During the early 1950s, an airstrip was built nearby and this helped start detailed exploration, excavation and restorations.

I have some very rare wildlife around me. You may meet over 50 white-nosed **coatis** moving together or several colourful flocks of keel-billed toucans, **Montezuma oropendolas** and brown jays. The screeches of howler monkeys compete with what may seem to you to be the roar of a jaguar. I am not silent at all as you can see. I am in the middle of a 357 sq km National Park.

I was the centre of the Mayan civilisation and trade. The Plaza Mayor, or Great Plaza, is perhaps my most stunning monument. The temple of the Giant Jaguar, a pyramid, is 145 ft high. The temple of Masks is another pyramid. My temples were both astrological observatories as well as sacrificial sites. My structure built in limestone is now stone-grey, but at one time, it was red, the colour of blood. My name means the 'centre of echoes'.

Mayan Temples, Tikal, North Guatemala

The fall of Tikal has various theories from an earthquake to a popular uprising. It is 1,000-year-old city that vanished within 100 years. It then remained buried for another 1,000 years in Guatemala's Petan region.

A pyramid at Tikal

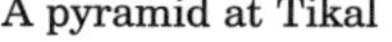

I am a temple dedicated to the oneness of all religions and mankind. My doors are open to people of all faiths, races and cultural backgrounds. Apart from the main prayer hall, I have an ancillary block with a reception centre, a library and an administrative building. I also have rest-rooms. My architect was Fariborz Sahba; Flint & Neill Partnership of London were the consultants; and Larsen & Toubro Limited were the contractors.

I am said to be an architectural wonder and am made of a combination of marble, cement, sand and dolomite. People of any faith can enter me to offer their prayers. I reach a height of more than 40 m. Fresh air, which is cooled as it passes over the fountains and pools, is drawn in through openings in the basement, up into the central hall, and expelled through a vent at the top of the interior dome. During the humid season a set of exhaust fans in the basement recycles air from the main hall into the cool basement and back.

I belong to the Baha'i sect and am now a significant landmark of my city. There are no clergymen in the temple and my service consists of prayers and readings of selections from Baha'i scriptures. The Baha'i religion is an independent one and not a sect of any other religion's manifestion. The Baha'is lay great emphasis on prayer and meditation. These, they believe, are important instruments for the progress of the human soul, both in this world and the next. The Baha'is pray to one God, the creator of the universe.

I am built in the shape of a half-opened lotus flower and was completed in 1986. I am said to be the Taj of modern India. I am surrounded by manicured lawns. I have 27 giant white petals, springing from nine pools and walkways signifying the nine unifying spiritual paths of the Baha'i faith. My petals consist of three folds of nine concrete portals, each covered outside with marble from Greece.

Lotus or Baha'i temple, New Delhi, India

The Baha'i temple or the Lotus temple is visited by over four million people annually. It is located on Bahapur hills and it is the seventh and most recent Baha'i house of worship in the world. It is the first Baha'i temple in Asia. The other temples are in Panama, Kampala, Illinois, Frankfurt, Sydney and West Samoa.

I am the holiest of all Shiva temples in my country. I am a square pagoda built on a single platform 23.6 m high. I have gold gilt doors on all the four sides. Inside I have a narrow walk around the sanctum of the *Shivalinga*. I am a UNESCO World Heritage Site. In the evening of ***Mahashivaratri***, the king of my country comes in a motocade with other members of the royal family to pay homage to my shrine.

The image of Lord Shiva in the form of ***jyotirlinga*** was covered with earth over the years, and soft green grass sprouted over it. As the legend goes, a cow used to come here mysteriously every day and offer her milk to this holy but hidden *linga* of Lord Shiva. When the owner finally came across the place where the cow used to offer her milk, he dug the place and found the *jyotirlinga* of Lord Shiva. After this, a number of cowherds gathered to worship this *linga* according to religious conformity, starting the tradition that is still followed today.

I was attacked and badly destroyed by Sultan Samsuddin of Bengal in the mid 14th century. I was damaged so badly that I had to be reconstructed. This was done only after 10 years by Javasimha Ramvardhana. Jyoti Malla renovated me again in AD 1416. Queen Gangadevi brought me to my present form during the reign of Shivasimha Malla. It is believed that in ancient times, Lord Shiva appeared at the site where I now stand as a forest deer and later as a flame.

The rulers of my country enriched me in their own ways through the centuries. According to *Gopalraj Vamsavali*, the oldest ever chronicle in my country, I was built by Supus Padeva, a Linchchhavi king. There is another chronicle which states that I was in the form of a *linga*-shaped *devalaya* before Supus Padeva converted me to a five-storeyed temple. It is also learnt that I was reconstructed by a king named Shivadeva. I was renovated by Ananta Malla, who added my two-tiered golden roof.

Pashupatinath temple, Kathmandu, Nepal

In the sanctum of the temple, there is a 3 ft high *Shivalinga* with four faces. All these faces have different names and significance. Pashupati is regarded as one of the most important places of pilgrimages for Hindus. Thousands of devotees from within and outside the country come to pay homage every day.

The four-faced *Shivalinga*

I am perhaps the greatest of all public gardens in the world. I have six green-houses of which two are especially enormous — the Palm House and the Temperate House. The Palm House was built in 1844-48, by engineer Richard Turner and architect Decimus Burton. It is a huge and beautiful iron-and-glass structure made of simple repeating units. The Temperate House, again by Decimus Burton, is bigger than the Palm House. It is 600 ft long and 60 ft high.

I have various important 19th-century structures apart from the large green-houses. I have a *pagoda* influenced by Japanese style. Various small Greek temples are dotted around me. In the Palm House are two lead figures, about 4 ft high, by John Cheere, of a shepherd and a shepherdess. Besides these are the 10 Queen's Beasts, carved by James Woodford in 1956, a monumental statue of an athlete struggling with a snake, and The Sower, an important work by Hamo Thornycroft. The figure of a peasant farmer is shown as a heroic figure.

My Marianne North Gallery was designed in Greek style by James Fergusson in 1882. It was built to display the botanical paintings of a 19th-century artist who travelled all over the world. Nearly 850 of Marianne North's oil paintings are on show in the original Victorian arrangement of 1882. The Economic Botany Collections, founded by the first official Director, Sir William Hooker, has 76,000 items, including world's finest wood collections (32,000 samples from 12,000 species) and thousands of bottles of oils.

My Aquatic Garden was first opened in 1909. Currently there are 116 different *taxa*; 40 of these are different varieties of waterlily, housed in the central tank. The planting plans for Decimus Burton's grand Broad Walk were designed by the famous English landscape architect William Andrews Nesfield in the 1840s. Designed in 1982, the Grass Garden replaced an Iris garden. Currently, there are 550 species of grasses grown in the Grass Garden

---

Kew Gardens, London, United Kingdom

On 30 July, 2003, the Royal Botanical Gardens was officially included as a World Heritage Site in the UNESCO list. A specimen of every known plant species is found here. It is probably the largest and most diverse living collection in the world.

A greenhouse

I am a living wonder. I have been developed and carved over 2,000 years with primitive handtools by Ifugao tribe. Erosion is my biggest threat today followed by the migration of many of my people, who prefer jobs in big cities to looking after me. I have been created by laying stones to build 'dams' on soil to hold back erosion. I am also called a 'stairway to the heavens'.

There is no electricity in the area I am seen. My people believe in ancestral spirits and chickens are often sacrificed. When one of my people dies, the body is hung for three days. Afterwards, the bones are placed inside the house so that the family can get support and good luck. My villagers make Bulul figures, or rice gods, to protect and increase the harvest. These are carved in male and female pairs, which are first bathed in animal blood before being placed outside the village rice-store during harvest time.

The watering system used for me is built with locally available material: bamboo tubes and elaborate mud channels. Despite my size, my people still need to buy rice from neighbouring provinces. To construct me, farmers first identify areas that are concave. Stones are placed around it and cracks in the slope are filled with gravel. More and more layers are added and the level of soil is raised. Some walls reach 6 m in height.

I am over 1,000 m tall. I have both old and new parts. My oldest parts are over 6,000-years old. I stretch across 49,400 acres along the Cordillera mountain range. I am essentially a landscape certified by experts to be a 'living testament of engineering and creative genius'. I am an UNESCO World Heritage Site. I am referred to as the eighth wonder of the world. I am 10 times larger than the Great Wall of China and I am higher than the world's tallest building.

Banaue Rice Terraces, Philippines

In 1994, then-President Fidel V. Ramos created the Ifugao Rice Terraces Commission (ITC). The ITC made plans for the restoration and preservation of the rice terraces, also helped by UNESCO, which invested an initial $15,000 in the ITC.

I am not one but comprise more than 1,000 objects. We were built in about the 8th century. We suddenly stopped being made in the 17th century. We are located on an island that is one of the most isolated places on the earth. Early settlers called the island 'Te Pito O Te Henua' ('navel of the world'). Experts are not sure as to who made us. We are said to be of Peruvian origin by some.

Our island was discovered by Polynesians in about AD 400. In addition to us, the island also has many **petroglyphs**, traditional wood carvings and *tapa* crafts. The early population flourished and as it kept increasing, forests were cleared for agriculture. We were also moved from our original places. We are so heavy that it is a wonder how people moved us. As the population kept increasing, our island saw civil wars and finally cannibalism.

The population of our island then started decreasing. Admiral Roggeveen discovered our island on Easter Day in 1722. After contact with the Western world, it saw slavery and disease and in 1800, the population became 111. The people, the island and the language are referred to locally as Rapa Nui. Today the population has risen and is stable.

We are giant head statues carved out of volcanic rock. Our island is the world's most isolated inhabited island. We have faced years of tropical rains and wind and are constantly under threat. Most of us weigh 14 tonnes and the largest amongst us, El Gigante, weighs over 140 tonnes and is 70 ft high. Experts are equally puzzled about how we were moved. Modern scientific teams have been working on our island trying various methods to find out how almost everything from pulling, lugging, tugging to cursing have been tried but with little success.

Moai Statues, Rapa Nui (Easter Island), Chile

Easter Island is over 2,000 miles from the nearest population centres, Tahiti and Chile, making it one of the most isolated places on the earth. Chile anexed it in 1888. Despite a growing Chilean presence, the island's Polynesian identity is still quite strong .

Among other things I am the world's largest estuarine forest. I am inhospitable and dangerous. Nearly 70 per cent of my area is under saline water. The only way to reach me is by motorised boats. It is believed that Bonbibi, my goddess, protects the wood-cutters, honey-collectors and fishermen that move around me despite the danger.

I am named after the tree species *Heritiera fomes*, locally called Sundari. I was named a UNESCO World Heritage Site in 1997. One of the projects going on inside me is the Bhagavatpur Crocodile Project. It is a breeding farm for salt-water crocodiles. I am can be divided into three zones, depending on the level of salt in the soil and water: a freshwater zone, a moderately saline zone and a saline zone.

I am the home of the Royal Bengal Tiger. I also have crocodiles, sharks and snakes. The Olive Ridley Turtle is also important for me and there is a conservation programme for them here. Though bird watching is not a common activity here, you can sometimes spot a swamp partridge, grey-headed lapwing, Pallas's fish-eagle, woodpeckers, tree pies or a mangrove whistler. The tigers that I have are maneaters and it is extremely dangerous to move around in me alone. Most of the areas are protected by wire-nets.

I am the only mangrove forest in the world. I cover 4,264 sq kms in India and a larger section in Bangladesh (60 per cent). A part of me, 2,585 sq kms, forms the largest Tiger Reserve and National Park in India. Visitors are not allowed within the National Park. I am a part of the world's largest delta formed by the rivers — Ganges, Brahmaputra and Meghna.

Sunderbans,
West Bengal, India

The tigers at the park are good swimmers. The National Park is home to 200 tigers. It is believed that the total number of tigers in India and Bangladesh is 400.

I am a city with the one of the largest mosques in India, Jami Masjid, built in AD 1571. To the left of the Jami Masjid, you will find my oldest mosque, the stone cutters' mosque. It is mainly built in red sandstone. Mughal Emperor Akbar planned me as his capital but abandoned me due to shortage of water. I was built between 1571-1585. Today I have a population of about 30,000 and can be called deserted. I still have retained many of the old structures.

The *Diwan-i-Aam* is the first hall of the royal palace. This hall was also used for celebrations and public prayers. I have a *Diwan-Khana-i-Khaas*, in the centre of which stands an intricately carved column supporting a huge bracketed capital. Four narrow causeways project from the centre and run to each corner of the chamber. I believe that Akbar's throne used to cover the circular space over the **capital** and his four ministers sat at the corners.

I have a pavilion called Panch Mahal with 176 differently carved pillars. The size of the floors decreases as you move up, so that each floor is smaller than the one below it. There is a single-domed kiosk on top supported by four columns. If you stand on top of the Panch Mahal, you can get a magnificent view of me and my surroundings. Many of my royal palaces have been built in Gujarati and Rajasthani architectural styles, using ornate columns, *jali* work, carving, and surface ornamentation.

You can enter me through the Buland Darwaza built in 1575. You need to climb up a 13-m flight of steps to enter the Buland Darwaza from outside. To the north of the Jami Masjid is the *dargah* of Sheikh Salim Chishti. Akbar built this in 1580-81, 80 years after the saint died. Childless women come here to ask for blessings of the saint. Akbar too was blessed with three sons here. I haven't travelled but I have heard that the lattice work in the *dargah* is among the finest in my country.

Fatehpur Sikri, Uttar Pradesh, India

Buland Darwaza was erected in AD 1602 to commemorate Akbar's victory over the Deccan. It is the highest gateway in India and ranks among the biggest in the world. Jami Masjid is one of the finest examples of Mughal architecture. It is said to be a copy of the mosque in Mecca and has designs derived from the Persian and Hindu architecture.

Panch Mahal

I am a cave shrine in the Trikuta mountains. I am said to have been built by the five Pandavas. I am about 98 ft long. The symbols of a large number of Hindu gods and goddesses can be seen in me. At the mouth of my original tunnel to the holy cave can be seen the symbols of Vakra Tunda Ganesha, Surya Dev and Chandra Dev.

According to legend, the goddess whose shrine I am wanted to get married to Lord Rama. He refused but at the same time he said he will be reborn in the Kaliyuga and marry her. He asked her to stay in a cave in the Trikuta hills where the three supreme goddesses were staying. He blessed her saying many devotees would come to visit her and she would be able to grant them their desires. He also sent Hanuman to serve her.

There are three natural shrines for Mahakali, Mahalakshmi and Mahasaraswati. I am believed to be the only place where the three *devis* are found in one temple. Earlier one needed to crawl into the cave through the *garba griha* over the *dhadh* of Bhairon Nath, who had chased the goddess and was ultimately killed by her. Today, due to a boon later given by her, a pilgrimage to her is not complete without a visit to the shrine of Bhairon higher up.

I can be reached on foot by a steep 13-km trek from the foot of the Trikuta hills, the same route that was followed by the goddess when fleeing from Bhairon. Thousands of devotees make the climb daily. It is said that only when she calls you, you can go to see her. It is also believed strongly by thousands that anything asked of the goddess with a true heart comes true.

Mata Vaishnodevi shrine, Jammu and Kashmir, India

It is said that evil forces had taken control of the world. The cries of devotees made Mahalakshmi, Mahakali and Mahasaraswati combine their powers to produce a goddess powerful enough to free the people of their suffering. The powerful goddess that they created is Vaishnodevi.

The shrine with Mata Vaishnodevi as in inset

I am an ancient religious site. The first habitation on me is from the Neolithic period. I am a rocky hill used for centuries for religious purposes. Goddess Athena was probably the first cult goddess for which I was used. The inscriptions on the numerous marble **korai**, bronze and clay statuettes and vases offered to her, indicate that the cult was established as early as 650-480 BC.

My monuments tell you about the different phases of history. Some of these were converted into Christian churches, and residences of the Franks and later of the Turks. The first excavations of me were conducted between 1835 and 1837. More systematic work was carried out between 1885-1890.

As you walk up me, you will see numerous small shrines, including one to the God Pan. During 450-330 BC, I saw three important temples erected on the ruins of earlier ones: the Parthenon, the Erechtheion, and the temple of Nike. The Propylaea, which is the grand entrance to me, was also constructed in the same period. It was designed by the architect Mnesikles. It comprises a central building and two lateral wings.

I am called the 'sacred rock'. My name means upper city. Many city-states of my country in ancient times were built around similar places as me, so that during times of invasion, people of the city could take refuge here. It is for this reason that the most sacred buildings of my city are on me. The city I am in is named after Goddess Athena.

Acropolis, Athens, Greece

It has a natural spring called the Klepsydra and a number of caves. Behind the Parthenon is the Acropolis Museum that has material from excavations on the hill. Founded in the mid 1800s, the museum was renovated between 1949 and 1953 and has nine exhibition rooms.

I am a symbol of my city. I have 102 floors and am 1,453 ft high. I was constructed in only two years — 1930 and 1931. I was dedicated as one of the Civil Engineering Monuments of the Millennium by the American Society of Civil Engineers in July 2001. I have three intercommunication systems connecting antennas to the transmitters on my upper floors.

On my 86th floor, at 1,050 ft, my observatory offers a panoramic view from within a glass-enclosed pavilion and from the surrounding open-air promenade. Since the observatory opened to the public in 1931, almost 110 million visitors have visited it, with over 3.5 million people annually. Apart from the observatory, I have the New York Skyride, a simulated helicopter ride and virtual-reality movie theatre. There are concerts and art exhibits in my lobby the year round. My Valentine's Day weddings are well known.

I am in over 90 movies, including *King Kong*, *Affair to Remember* starring Cary Grant and Deborah Kerr, *Sleepless in Seattle* starring Tom Hanks and Meg Ryan, When *Harry met Sally*, starring Meg Ryan. In July 1945, a US B-25 bomber crashed into my 79th floor office of the Catholic War Relief Services. As many as 14 people died.

I am once again the tallest skyscraper in my city as I was for 40 years until the World Trade Center was built. My Art Deco lobby, a five-storey masterpiece is lined in 10,000 sq ft of marble and rich granite. It has stainless steel to offset the stones. It is strange to believe that I was built in the middle of the Depression. My façade is made of more than 200,000 cu ft of Indiana limestone and granite.

The Empire State Building, New York City, USA

This is New York's most famous structure standing at Fifth Avenue and 34th Street. President Hoover inaugurated the building by pressing a button in the White House that switched on the lights in this building.

I am the youngest volcano in the Western Hemisphere. I exploded out of a cornfield. Within a year, my cinder cone reached 1,100 ft. Within two years, my slow-moving lava flows buried most of the town after which I am named and partially buried a neighbouring town. First exploding in 1943, I continued till 1952. My lava eventually covered about 25 sq km.

I still let a little hot gas escape sometimes but I am more or less dead. I am one of over 1,000 vents in the Michoacan-Guanajuato monogenetic field. This is an area where there are hundreds of vents scattered about, instead of a single big volcano. Each of these vents erupts only once. Even though I am almost dead, another vent might suddenly pop up near me.

Most of my activity was during the first year of the eruption. Even though my cinder cone continued to grow for another eight years, only another 290 ft was added. I erupted much less violently after this initial bout and again during the last six months I became violent. Despite everything, no one was killed by my lava or ash. Three people were killed by lightning associated with my eruption.

I am considered important because it was the first time modern people were able to observe a volcano working from the beginning to the 'end'. I did not harm people but destroyed their fields and crops. I am the fastest growing volcano ever recorded in history. I grew up to 150 ft in just six days. After I covered the town, the only visible building was the top of the church steeple.

Paricutin Volcano, Mexico

Paricutin poured out over 1 billion tonnes of lava during its nine-year life span. The Paricutin is a cinder-cone volcano. The cones of such volcanos are formed from cinders, which are small, jagged pieces of rock and ash. When a cinder cone volcano erupts, these small cinders are scattered all over.

I am a temple with a diference, carved out of solid basalt rock. I am a representation of Mount Kailash, the abode of Lord Shiva. I am open from three sides. In my large hall I have nine sculptured panels representing Lord Shiva in different moods. I am designed very symmetrically in a geometric **mandala**.

I was perhaps built by the Silhara kings belonging to the period between 9th-12th centuries. According to legend, it was Pulkesin ll, the great warrior-prince of Chalukya dynasty, who built me to celebrate his victory over the Kalchuri king, Krishnaraja. At the centre of the back wall, a shrine was introduced for Buddha's image. I am probably built by the same families of craftsmen and sculptors who worked in Ellora.

Even though I am a cave, the pillars inside me give an impression that they support my roof. My panels show Shiva practicing yoga, Shiva meditating with snakes coiled around his neck, and Shiva with his wife, Parvati. Panel 6 of the caves represents the marriage of Shiva with Parvati with the rites being performed by Brahma and scores of other gods attending the marriage. Panel 5 of the cave describes the coming of Ganga from the heaven to the earth.

I am a UNESCO World Heritage Site. The island I am on also has the same name. My island has been a commercial, military and religious centre for centuries and has traces of early Buddhist culture. The film based on E.M. Foster's '*A Passage to India*' was shot at my site.

Elephanta Caves, Maharashtra, India

When the Portuguese conquered the Elephanta Island, they first found a monolith elephant and hence the island was named Elephanta. It is believed that the caves were used for target practice. This has destroyed many of the sculptures. The British later captured the island. The monolith elephant is now kept in the Bombay Museum.

I was built in three or four stages beginning in the 8th or 9th millennium BC to sometime in 1100 BC. My original purpose is unclear but people feel I was a temple for the worship of ancient gods. I am also thought to be an astronomical observatory in the prehistoric era. Still others feel that I was a sacred site for the burial of high-ranking citizens.

I am ancient and my construction is thus an engineering feat. Initially there was a bank-and-ditch arrangement, constructed approximately 5,000 years ago. The ditch was dug with tools made from the antlers of red deer and wood. There was an underlying layer of chalk that was shovelled with tools made from the shoulder blades of cattle.

Today many of my original stones have fallen or been removed over the ages for use in home construction or road repair. There has been serious damage to some of the smaller **bluestones** from tourists who try to minutely examine them. Close examination, like touching, etc. is prohibited since 1978. The prehistoric carvings on my larger **sarsen** stones show signs of significant wear.

I am a megalith, a group of standing stones arranged in a circle. There are many theories about who built me, including the Druids, Greeks, Phoenicians, and Atlanteans. My first stone circle, which is now the inner circle, comprised of small bluestones and is believed to be from the Prescelly mountains. I was built about 2,000 BC. My huge stones are capped by 30 **lintels**, or equally mammoth stones across the top. I give the impression of huge doorways. The bank-and-ditch arrangement is called *henge.*

Stonehenge, Wiltshire, England, United Kingdom

England has a large number of megaliths with names like Avebury, the Hurlers, the Merry Maidens, and the Rollright Stones. The name 'Stonehenge' means 'hanging stones'.

I was originally built as a fortification structure by three states: Yan, Zhao and Qin. I was built, repaired, reconstructed with the passing dynasties. Emperor Qin Shihuang was the one who joined me together to fend off the invasions from the Huns in the north after the unification of my country. A popular legend says that a certain section of me collapsed because of the bitter sorrow and weeping by Meng Jiangnu, after her husband died during my construction. This legend has been spread widely through textbooks, folk songs and traditional operas.

I was built by locally available material. A great army of manpower, composed of soldiers, prisoners and local people, built it. I am one of the greatest wonders in the world. In 1987, I was included in the UNESCO World Heritage list. I am the world's largest military structure. I have an average height of 10 m and a width of 5 m.

I start from Shanhaiguan Pass in the east to Jiayuguan Pass in the west traversing provinces of Liaoning, Hebei, Beijing, Tianjin, Shanxi, inner Mongolia, Ningxia, Shaanxi and Gansu. I got my present form during the Ming dynasty. They enlarged my brick and granite work and sophisticated designs were added. My watchtowers were redesigned and modern canons were mounted in strategic areas.

I am a landmark of the earth and according to popular belief, I am visible from the moon. According to astronauts Neil Armstrong, Jim Lovell and Jim Irwin, I am not. However, I am the only man-made structure visible from outer space. I run 6,700 km from east to west across five provinces. When I was first being joined together, under the direction of General Meng Tian over a period of 10 years during the Qin dynasty, a labour force of 3,00,000 was used.

Great Wall of China, China

The wall can be seen in a relatively natural state at Simatai, 110 km north-east of Beijing. This part of the wall has not been developed into a popular tourist attraction due to its distance and less public transportation options. Locally the wall is known as '*Wan-Li Qang-Qeng*' or the 10,000-Li Long Wall (10,000 *li* = 5,000 km).

I am a city in Germany. I have one of the most beautiful settings in all Europe, surrounded by green hills, forests and vineyards. I have many interesting sights including two city chateaux. I am also a top venue for hit musicals like *Dance of the Vampires* and *Phantom of the Opera*.

My most beautiful square in the city centre is Schlossplatz. The central part of the Neues Schloss or New Palace today houses rooms for the representatives of the State Government while the side wings accommodate two ministries. I have Europe's biggest zoo and botanical garden, Wilhelma. I also have the Mercedes Benz and Porsche museums of the world's oldest car manufacturer and the famous sports car manufacturer respectively.

One of my important landmarks is the Fernsehturm, which is the world's first broadcasting tower made of steel-reinforced concrete. The Bohnenviertel in my older part has wine bars, popular pubs and antique shops.

The beautiful and varied countryside around me, for example in the Swabian forest and around the three Kaiserberg peaks in the Siebenmühlen valley, is a paradise for walks and hikes. The Baroque Schloss in Ludwigsburg with Baroque Fairy-Tale and Flower Garden is an enchanting place. There is also the Maulbronn Abbey, the most completely preserved monastic complex north of the Alps, now included on the UNESCO World Cultural Heritage list.

Stuttgart, Germany

It is a paradise for art lovers. There are more than 40 theatres, 30 art galleries and numerous museums, including car museums, the wine-growing museum, the Hegel House, the Linden Ethnology Museum and the Carl Zeiss planetarium.

Wilhelma Zoo

I was originally just a fort and the capital of my province was in Dhar. Towards the end of the 13th century, I came under the rule of the Sultans of Malwa. The first of these kings renamed me Shadiabad, the 'city of joy'. I was captured by the Delhi Sultanate, by Ala-ud-din Khilji in AD 1305. The first buildings that came up were mosques, built with pillars taken from Hindu temples, similar to other places of conquest.

I am encircled by 45 km of walls with 12 gateways. The most famous of my gates is the Delhi Darwaza, which also serves as my main entrance. To enter me, you will come through a series of gateways, armed with walled enclosures and bastions. Some of my other gateways are the Rampol Darwaza, Jehangir Gate and Tarapur Gate. The Jami Masjid near the centre of my plateau is one of the finest creations of the Ghori dynasty. It is said that it was inspired by the mosque of Damascus.

I also have the tomb of Hoshang Shah, India's first marble edifice and one of the supreme examples of Afghan architecture. Shah Jahan sent some of his architects, among them was Ustad Hamid, who was associated with the Taj Mahal, to study the design. The Jahaz Mahal built by Mahmud Khilji is between two water bodies, the Kaphur Talao and the Munja Talao. I always feel that the building is floating on water. Probably this is why its name is literally the 'ship palace'.

I am a celebration of the love of Baz Bahadur and Rani Roopmati. From her pavilion on the hill, I saw Rani Roopmati every day, looking down on Baz Bahadur's palace and the Narmada river. Baz Bahadur's palace was constructed in the early 6th century. It has a spacious courtyard fringed with halls and high terraces which give a terrific view of the lovely surroundings. It is said that if you haven't visited me during the monsoons, your life's experience is not complete.

Mandu,
Madhya Pradesh, India

The Rewa Kund is a reservoir built by Baz Bahadur, equipped with an aqueduct to supply Roopmati's palace with water. Rani Roopmati's Pavilion was built as an army observation post but it served as Roopmati's retreat. From this pavilion perched on a hilltop, the queen could gaze at the Narmada flowing by, just like she did at her father's home and without looking at which she could not eat her food.

I am a modern wonder. I was not a new idea. The first survey was by King Charles I of Spain, who wanted to create a shortcut to the Pacific Ocean instead of the dangerous and long journey around Cape Horn. However, no plans are made to build me. The first 'practical' idea was by Ferdinand de Lesseps, who is connected with the Suez Canal in Egypt.

Despite much publicity, the stock of Lesseps' company, *Compagnie Universelle du Canal Interoceanique* only managed to raise 30 million francs of his estimated 400 million francs. The French Canal Company worked for several years, but increasing costs, unseen engineering problems and bouts of yellow fever killed hundreds of workers and the project eventually ended in 1889. The French now looked for a buyer, which turned out to be USA.

Under President Theodore Roosevelt, USA started building me. I was considered important for their world trade. My country was under the Colombian government, who demanded payment from USA. This nearly stopped work on me. However, my country became independent and my government agreed on the project. President Roosevelt became the first American President to travel abroad while in office and when he came to visit me, he saw how my work was progressing.

I was inaugurated in 1914, after 10 years. The total amount spent on me was $387 million. Ships could now sail from the Atlantic Ocean to the Pacific Ocean through me. I however became a source of anxiety and fights and two treaties were signed between the USA and my country in 1977. According to these treaties, I was handed over to my country unofficially on 14 December 1999, and officially on 31 December 1999.

The Panama Canal, Panama

The building of the canal involved several engineering problems. Army Lieutenant George Washington Goethals was the third American head of the project, and it was he who actually turned it around. Unlike the Suez Canal, which is a **sea-level canal**, the Panama Canal is a **lock canal**. The most difficult area was at Culebra Mountain-Culebra Cut.

I am the result of an idea that first oiginated during the age of the Pharaohs. They did build my predecessor, which was later rebuilt by the Greeks, followed by the Romans. There is some confusion as to whether my very first ancestor was built during the reign of Tuthmosis III or Pharaoh Necho. I transport 14 per cent of the total world trade, 26 per cent of oil exports, 41 per cent of the total volume of goods and cargo that reach Arab Gulf ports.

Napoleon's engineers revived the idea of building me. I was to be a link between the Red Sea and the Mediterranean Sea. The French engineers showed a difference in level of 10 m between both seas, and it was calculated that if I was built under such circumstances, a large area would be flooded. However, the calculations were found to be wrong, and work began on me in 1859. I was finally built under the French Consul in Cairo and the engineer Ferdinand de Lesseps. I am 167 km long.

The workers that were used to build me were practically treated as slaves. Of more than 2.4 million workers, more than 125,000 lost their lives. I was completed around 1867, and on 17 November 1869, I was officially inaugurated. My inauguration was a grand affair with royalty of many nations present. An Opera House was built, and Verdi was commissioned to compose his famous opera, *Aida* was for the opening ceremony. However, Verdi could not complete it on time and *Aida* was premiered at the Opera a year later.

I can accommodate huge ships, 500 m long and 70 m wide. Today my capacity is more than 25.000 vessels annually. From July 1956, I became a national canal. This was announced by my country's President, Abdul Gamal Nasser. His decision came as a result of the refusal by the British, French and American governments for a loan for building the Aswan High Dam. He claimed that I would provide the money to do this. Great Britain, France and Israel immediately invaded my country, but Nasser was eventually victorious.

The Suez Canal, Egypt

In 1967, Israel occupied the Sinai Peninsula, and the canal was a buffer zone. The canal was reclaimed during the 1973 Arab-Israeli war, and the re-opening ceremony took place in 1975. Today, approximately 50 ships cross the canal daily. The Suez Canal shortens the distance between East and West considerably.

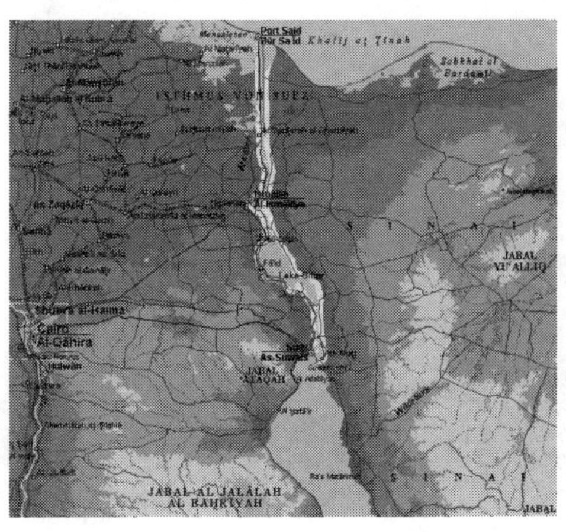

A map of the Suez Canal

I am a palace complex called Gu Gong locally. I am rectangular in shape and I am the world's largest palace complex. I cover 74 hectares with 9,999 buildings inside me. I am surrounded by a 6 m deep moat and a 10 m high wall. I am a UNESCO Heritage Site since 1987. I am one of the most popular tourist attractions.

My construction began in 1407 and was completed 14 years later. A million workers, including a 100 thousand artisans were involved in building me. The stone used for me was quarried from Fangshan. It was said that wells were dug every 50 m along the road in order to pour water onto the road in winter to slide huge stones of ice into me. Huge amounts of timber and other materials were got from faraway provinces.

Since yellow is the symbol of the royal family, I am primarily yellow in colour. The palaces inside me have roofs of yellow glazed tiles; yellow decorations are seen on the walls, and even the bricks on the ground are made yellow. However, Wenyuange, the royal library, has a black roof. The reason is that it was believed black represented water and could extinguish fire, which signifies a source of danger for books.

I am divided into two parts: the southern section or the Outer Court and the northern section or the Inner Court. The Outer Court was for business and the Inner Court was the residence of the royal family. Fourteen emperors of the Ming dynasty and 10 emperors of the Qing dynasty had reigned here till 1924 when the last Emperor was driven from the Inner Court. The film, *The Last Emperor* and the book tell you much about life within my walls. I have numerous rare treasures and curiosities. I am to the north of Tiananmen Square.

Forbidden City, Beijing, China

It is now known as the Palace Museum and is open to tourists. Splendid painted decorations on the palaces, the grand and deluxe halls, with their magnificent treasures thrill the tourist and genuine art lovers.

I am a mountain peak. Italy's Reinhold Messner has climbed me twice without oxygen, and once in four days. He is also the first to climb me alone in 1980. In 1970, Yuichiro Miura of Japan was the first person to descend me on skis. The first disabled person to attempt me was American, Tom Whittaker, who climbed with a prosthetic leg to 24,000 ft in 1989, 28,000 ft in 1995, and finally reached my summit in 1998. Ang Rita, who has reached the summit 10 times, holds the record for the most number of ascents.

I am also known as Sagarmatha, Chomolangma and Qomolangma Feng. I am 29,035 ft high. My elevation was determined using **GPS satellite** equipment on 5 May 1999. Earlier I was thought to be a bit lower. I was formed about 60 million years ago. More than 600 climbers from 20 countries have climbed to my summit by various routes, from both north and south. At least 100 people have died while attempting me, most commonly by avalanches, falls in crevasses, cold, or because of thin air.

In the first seven attempts, a route to the summit via the **North Col** and **North Ridge** seemed possible. All were unsuccessful. George Mallory, who spearheaded the first three expeditions, lost his life with Andrew Irvine during a failed ascent in 1924. Unsuccessful attempts continued through 1938, then halted during World War II. With the war's end, Tibet had closed its borders, and the country I am actually in did the opposite.

In 1953 Edmund Hillary and Tenzing Norgay reached my summit. In 1975, Junko Tabei of Japan was the first woman to reach my summit. I was once known as K 15 and have been subsequently named, in 1865, after the British Surveyor-General of India, who was the first person to record the height and location. I am the highest mountain peak in the world.

Mount Everest, Nepal

Climbing on Everest is very strictly regulated by both Nepalese and Chinese governments. On the north side, a Buddhist monastery stands at the foot of the Rongbuk glacier. In 1975, China tackled Everest with a 410-member team, the largest team ever.

I am one of the world's most impressive archaeological sites, a fortress-city high up in the mountains. I was built by the Incas on the summit of the 'Old Peak', overlooking the deep canyon of the Urubamba river. Although the Inca population was only about 1,00,000, they ruled over 10 million people from different ethnic groups. The Inca did not leave written records and Spanish chronicles make no mention of me. I am thus a mystery.

I was discovered only in 1911 by the American professor, Hiram Bingham. I am thought to be a sanctuary or temple that was inhabited by high priests and by women who were dedicated to the gods. Of the 135 skeletons found, 109 were of women. Next to me is the Great Central Temple, a three-walled building with fine stonework and an attached smaller temple. I am believed to be built by the second Inca king, more than 500 years ago.

I was most likely a royal estate and religious retreat. Today when you enter the Emperor's residence near me, you will find a scene of the ancient times. You will hear the natural sounds as you would have during those times and a conversation in Quechua, the language of the Incas. I have 200 buildings, most being residences. Advanced terracing and irrigation methods were used to cultivate maize and potatoes. I am a hiker's paradise, and of course a UNESCO World Heritage Site.

Hiram Bingham found many objects of stone, bronze, ceramic and obsidian inside me but no gold or silver, as was expected after the finds of life-size gold replicas of maize and other plants in the temple of the Sun, an Inca temple. Intially it was thought that the Spaniards who invaded Inca land looted me but this wasn't true because they never discovered me. Wars between rival Inca tribes or epidemics are two possible reasons for my decline. Whatever be the reason, I was most probably abandoned by the Incas before Spanish conquest.

Inca city of Machu Picchu, Peru

Machu Picchu is a city located high in the Andes mountains in modern Peru. More than 3,00,000 people visit it every year. Needless to say, all the tourist activity is putting enormous pressure on the site. The fee to hike the trail was increased from $17 to $50, and it is compulsory for hikers today to trek with a registered guide.

On 15 April 1996, I was procaimed to be the tallest building in the world, surpassing Chicago's Sears Tower, by the Council on Tall Buildings. I was developed by a group of private investors in association with the government of my country and the national oil company. American architect Cesar Pelli designed me with twin towers with a height to width ratio of 9:4.

I am supported by 75×75-ft concrete cores and an outer ring of columns. I have 14,000-22,000 sq ft of column-free office space per floor. A human '*Spider Man*' from France once attempted to scale the outside of the building without the help of ropes. The police didn't attempt to apprehend him on the way up and just coolly waited to arrest him at the top.

My underground car park was designed to accommodate up to 10,000 vehicles. However, the architects forgot that since there were mainly offices inside me, most people would be leaving at the same time. The crowd would have been so huge that by the time the last person was able to get out, it would have almost been time to turn around and go back into work again. Thus, a network of underground narrow tunnels were built to allow traffic to move out more systematically. A huge extra area was thus left behind which had to be cabled off.

Pelli used Islamic arabesques and repetitive geometric structures characteristic of Muslim architecture to build me. Each tower's floor plan forms an eight-pointed star, formed by intersecting squares; curved and pointed bays create a scalloped facade to denote temple towers. I have 88 storeys and am 1,483 ft tall. A flexible skybridge joins my towers on the 42nd floor. There are 10 escalators and 76 elevators for both the buildings combined.

Petronas Towers, Kuala Lumpur, Malaysia

It took 36,910 tonnes of steel to build the towers. It takes 90 seconds to travel from the basement parking lot to the top of each tower. Together, the towers have 32,000 windows. It takes window washers an entire month to wash each tower just once!

At 3,776 m, I am my country's highest mountain. I am actually a volcano that has been worshipped as a sacred mountain. I am very popular in literature, painting and other arts. The most renowned work is by a Ukiyo-e painter, Hokusai. Accordng to a local proverb, he who climbs me once is a wise man; he who climbs me twice is a fool. Earlier women were not allowed to climb my summit because my goddess would have been jealous of other women.

I am currently classified as active with low risk of eruption. My last recorded eruption occurred in 1707 during the **Edo period**. A new crater along with a second peak, Hoeizan, formed halfway down my side. My name can be said to denote 'wealth' and '**samurai**'. Since recorded history, more than 10 eruptions have created my present form.

Although I appear to be a single symmetrical cone, I am far more complex than you might guess. I am actually made up of three superimposed volcanoes: Komitake, Kofuji, and Shinfuji. I originated from Fossa Magna, which was formed almost along with the country I am in. After that, Mikasa Sanchi was formed by the eruption of Komitake. Kofuji volcano's repeated eruptions covered the Komitake volcano. The Shinfuji volcano was active for a long time until my recent form appeared.

If you look at me closely, you will realise that I am not perfect. For example, a slight bump on the northern slope of the mountain, at about 7,550 ft, is part of the summit crater of Komitake, the oldest of the three volcanoes. It was active in the Middle Pleistocene period. Kofuji or older Fuji was active 80,000-10,000 years ago.

Mount Fuji, Honshu, Japan

Mount Fuji is located in Yamanashi and Shizuoka. It can be seen from Tokyo and Yokohama in clear weather.

I was a calculated and well thought of project. For more than two decades before I was built, the benefits that I would give were obvious: the hydroelectric power would be enormous, I would be an antidote to the cycles of drought and flood in the southwest of my country. I was also vital for the growth of major cities near me for water and power supply. Though my construction began only in 1931, the site testing had begun in the early 1920s.

My project was passed via the Swing-Johnson bill in 1927. A conglomerate of six companies won the job with a bid for $48,890,955. Because my site was so remote, before work could begin, roads and railroad lines had to be laid. The Colorado river, across which I was built, was diverted through four diversion tunnels. Engineers calculated that the concrete used to build me would take over 100 years to cool and then I would crack. To avoid this, concrete was poured in blocks and refrigerated water was then pumped through the blocks in pipes.

I was completed in 1935. Power generation began in 1936. I was earlier called as Boulder Canyon Project even though I was built on the Black Canyon. I impound the waters of Lake Mead, the largest reservoir in my country. My water is used to irrigate more than 263,000 hectares in states of my country and 162,000 hectares in Mexico. I am a major supplier of hydroelectric power and help in flood control, river regulation and improved navigation.

As 726 ft high and 1,244 ft long, I am one of the world's largest dams. I was commissioned by the Bureau of Reclamation of my country. I am named after one of my Presidents who took an active part in building me.

Hoover Dam, Arizona/Nevada, USA

The dam was dedicated to the nation on 30 September 1935. President Franklin D. Roosevelt called the Hoover Dam "an engineering victory of the first order — another great achievement of American resourcefulness, skill, and determination." It is named after Herbert Hoover.

I am the biggest temple in a complex with groups of temples built from AD 879-1191 at the height of the **Khmer** civilisation. My kings ruled a huge area, almost comprising entire Southeast Asia, from the great **citadel** here. There are more than 100 temples in this complex. The temples are the only surviving remains of my glorious civilisation. The other buildings were all built of wood and thus have decayed and gone.

My city was discovered by Henri Mahout in 1860. It was shrouded in mystery earlier, broken down later by the deciphering of my scripts. Khmer architecture had a definite style. A number of well-planned buildings surround many central shrines. These buildings or temples were set around courtyards and each courtyard was linked by avenues. The less important buildings were located at the outer edges of the complex, with the most important ones and the shrines in the centre.

The temples in my complex are single brick towers with one dooor. The doorway was often made of stone which was carved with simple designs. Inside was a small room in which was kept the statue representing the God, usually Shiva or Vishnu. **Laterite** and sandstone were the main building materials. When larger temples were built, the stone doorways were carved for decoration. Sandstone, which is very easily carved, was used. The smaller Beng Mealear temple, built shortly before me, is considered as my blue-print.

I was built by Suryavaram II to honour Lord Vishnu during the first half of the 12th century, as the king was identified with Vishnu. I was also intended as the king's burial site. I have five central shrines surrounded by a moat and three galleries. *Apsaras* are found on the walls of all my galleries. I was constructed over a period of 30 years and covering an area of about 81 hectares. When the Khmer Empire declined, I was turned into a Buddhist temple. In 1992, I and my entire city was declared a UNESCO World Heritage Site and was also put on the list of World Heritage in Danger.

Angkor Wat, Cambodia

The city of Angkor is located over 192 miles from Cambodia's capital, Phnom Penh. After the discovery by Mahout, research efforts continued until 1968, when the Vietnam war disrupted the studies. The Khmer Rouge, an extreme Left organisation which runs guerrilla activities cut tourism down. The guerrilla movement killed a number of Buddhist monks who were staying at Angkor.

I am a Gothic-style Benedictine abbey based on a rocky islet. I am known as the 'wonder of the West'. Dedicated to St. Michael, I was built between the 11th and 16th centuries. What I am today is all because of Abbot Hildebert, whose ambitious plan for me started in 1020. Instead of removing the rock to make a level base for my church, he added a foundation to make a level base, and built from there.

In the early 8th century, the Archangel Michael apeared to Bishop Aubert of Avranges, who built my first chapel. In 966, a Benedictine monastery was established here, and the church was started to be reconstructed. The church was burnt and Abbot Hildebert II began my Abbey church from 1023, during the time of Richard II. I gradually began to move away from religion and by the late 18th century, I became a prison! In 1874, my country's government assumed responsibility for my upkeep and restoration.

My church was completed in 1153, but Abbot Roger II continued to plan and now built a tri-level gallery/ cloister/ dormitory. When the Duke of Brittany accidentally set fire to my church in 1203, Phillip Augustus used his influence to get funds from the king of my country to repair my buildings. Instead of repairs, Abbot Jordan built 'The Merveille' with a number of great halls, kitchens, cloisters, and a dormitory, which took 20 years.

Hildebert's original foundation was not adequate for suppoting the weight of the later constructions. In 1300, one of my towers collapsed, followed in 1421 by the collapse of Hildebert's nave. Reconstruction started in 1450 and was completed only by 1521. I am built on a strong rock that is 84 m high. I was aiso a sanctuary and became a symbol of the Allies landing in my city during the Second World War. I was added to UNESCO's World Heritage List in 1979.

Mont St. Michael, Normandy and Brittany, France

The buildings of Mont St. Michael are constructed of granite, but there is some limestone too. During the hundred years' war, the fortifications of Mont St. Michael were reinforced. The fortifications include **crenellated ramparts**, towers and a 14th-century **barbican**.

I am an engineering miracle. I am 11,811 ft long, 3215 ft thick at the base and 364 ft tall. I provide irrigation and electricity for my entire country. When built, I created across Lake Nasser a huge reservoir. I increased cultivable land in my country by 30 per cent and raised the water-table. I doubled my country's available electricity supply. I was built in the 1960s, supplementing an older counterpart.

I have 18 times the material used in the Great Pyramid of Cheops. The lake I created is some 500 miles long and at the time it was built, it was the world's largest artificial lake. As the waters of Lake Nasser began to rise when I was nearing completion, the temples of Abu Simbel, a set of two temples constructed for Ramses II during the 13th century BC, were cut from the rock and shifted to higher ground.

Before I was built, the population in my country was fast outrunning the agricultural production, and it was clear that the great river flowing through the country had to be controlled for agricultural development. This also meant hydroelectric power, which was very essential for industry. My older counterpart, the Old Dam, commenced in 1899. Its height was raised in subsequent building phases in 1907-12 and 1929-34. However, the reservoir area was insufficient. I thus became necessary.

My designs were drawn in the 1950s. The nationalisation of the Suez Canal funded my construction. USSR designed my earth structure and provided the equipment required to build my power station. I was inaugurated in 1970 by President Sadat. Because of me, my country did not have to blink an eyelid during the drought that hit my continent during the late 1980s and again came to the rescue by preventing several floods in my country in the 1990s.

High Dam, Aswan, Egypt

The reservoir of the High Dam, *El Saad al Aali*, began filling in 1964 while the dam was still under construction. A rescue operation was begun in 1960 under UNESCO and the entire Abu Simbel site was dismantled and reassembled in a new location, 65 m higher and 200 m behind the river.

I am a rushing water body that flows off a table-top mountain and freely falls 2,421 ft to the river below. My table-top mountain is one of the many in the region. The natives call it a *tepuyi*. My particular *tepuyi* is called 'Auyantepui'. My waters fall into the Canon del Diablo (devil's canyon).

I am a part of the Parque Nacional Canaima, my country's second largest park. There are two ways to see me: one is from the air in an airplane; the second is by a trek upstream the Carrao river, and then the Churun river, and then through the jungle. The village of Canaima is the major gateway to me. Even Canaima is not connected well by land to other parts of the country. Most people fly to Canaima and then take a light plane or boat to me.

Before I got my present name, I was called the Churun Meru. You can also enjoy me from the Raton Island. I am on the Carrao river, a tributary of the Caroni river. I am a cataract waterfall. I was discovered in 1910 by a Spanish explorer called Ernesto Sanchez La Cruz. My *tepuyi* mountain is considered to be one of my country's most important biological reserves, with over 800 plant species. Of these, 77 per cent are endemic.

I am the tallest waterfall on the earth. In total, I am 15 times higher than Niagara Falls. I am named after Jimmy Angel, a pilot from Missouri who first saw me in 1933. He returned in 1937 and landed on top of my *tepuyi*. His plane remained with me for 33 years. Angel and his wife and two other people with them, managed to climb down the *tepuyi*. His original plane today is in the Aviation Museum in Maracay and on top of me is a replica that you can still see.

Angel Falls, Venezuela

Tepuyis were formed out of sandstone billions of years ago. The Angel Falls mesa is one of over a 100 of its kind which are scattered about the Guiana Highlands of south-east Venezuela.

I am a part of the Jefferson National Expansion Memorial Park, which was established on 21 December 1935. This park cost the government of my country and my city $30 million; my individual cost came to less than US$ 15 million. I am a modernistic 'sculpture', 630 ft high. My construction began on 12 February 1963, and was finished on 28 October 1965. I was opened to the public from 24 July 1967.

I am designed by architect Eero Saarinen. Saarinen had submitted my design in a competition in 1947 and wanted a shape that was slightly elongated and thinner towards the top — a shape that produces a subtle soaring effect and transfers more of the structure's weight downward rather than outward at the base. I am made of stainless steel and am 630 ft tall. I have a 60-ft deep foundation and cover 630 ft at ground level.

I am my nation's highest memorial. My top sways 0.5–1 ins in 20 mph wind. My legs are equilaterial triangles, narrowing from 54 ft in at the base to 17 ft at the top. Each wall consists of a stainless steel skin covering reinforced concrete from ground level to 300 ft or carbon steel and rebar from 300 ft to the peak. My interior is hollow and contains a unique transport system leading to an observation deck at the top.

Underneath me is a visitor's centre with a Museum of Westward Expansion, exhibiting the history of the St. Louis riverfront, tram loading areas, a movie theatre showing a documentary on my construction, and a movie theatre with a rotating playlist. I am a **catenary** arch. You can take a tram to my top with five people to a car. The tram moves at a rate of 240 ft per minute. There are thankfully not many emergencies, for if there were, you would have needed to climb down 1,076 steps.

Gateway Arch, St. Louis, USA

The arch commemorates the purchase of Lousiana by USA and the western expansion of the country. Similar to Saarinen's Ingalls' Hockey Rink at Yale and his TWA terminal, the arch is Saarinen's last great feat. Although it was estimated that 13 people would die while building it (according to a cost:death ratio), no deaths occurred.

I am a temple in a mysterious, enchanting and little known city of the Mayan civilisation. The buldings of my city were made of limestone and painted in many different colours. I am a memorial to a king, K'inich Janaab' Pakal ('Pacal the Great'), who also built me himself. I probably have the grandest sarcophagus known outside ancient Egypt.

My city became known only in 1773, and then got rediscovered and lost several times. It, and with it I, was finally definitely discovered in 1841 by explorers Stephens and Catherwood, who wrote about my city, drew splendidly and introduced the world to me and vice versa. Of an estimated 500 structures that are scattered around me in my city, only 34 have been opened.

I was born to be a burial chamber, the only one of my kind, into the buildings discovered so far. From my top, there is a stairway that moves down to my tomb. My site was probably occupied from as early as 300 BC. It became a major population centre only about AD 600. I and most other buildings were constructed between mahogany, cedar and sapodilla trees.

I am named thus because of the **hieroglyphic** texts found on my inner walls. This is the most extensive surviving Maya inscription. I am a pyramid-like structure, made up of nine receding divisions. The front stairway is divided into an ascending series of 9, 19, 19, 13 and 9 steps, making a total of 69 stairs to the top. Interestingly, it was in his 69th year of reign that K'inich Janaab' Pakal died.

The Temple of Inscriptions, Palenque, Mexico

The sarcophagus and its covering slab were sculptured first. The pyramid was built from the base up after the crypt was finished. It is the grandest memorial to a single person in Central America.

I am an island nation, fast becoming a major tourist destination. Three of my capitals are named World Heritage Sites by the UNESCO. My chief crop is rice. Tea, rubber and coconut are also important agricultural crops. Tea gets me a lot of foreign revenue. Other important crops and spices are cocoa, cinnamon, cardamom, nutmeg, pepper and cloves. My first settlers were the nomadic Veddahs. Legends say that they were the demonic *yakshas*, conquered by my kings.

Anuradhapura was my first capital founded in 5th century BC. Polonnaruwa was the medieval capital and Kandy was the last capital under the kings of my nation. UNESCO launched a project called Cultural Triangle in 1978 to restore the monuments located in these cities. Marco Polo considered me the finest island of my size in the entire world.

My biodiversity is said to be greater per sq km of surface area than that of any other country in the Asian region. My longest river is Mahaweli, which is 335 km. I was invaded on and off and my capital was also shifted until the Portuguese arrived on my shores in 1505. They came to trade in spices but stayed on to rule, followed by the Dutch. The Dutch were displaced by the British. I gave the world its first female Prime Minister Sirimavo.

I am a tiny island 65,610 sq km in extent, located just 35 km away from the southern tip of another country. My capital today is Sri Jayawardanepura Kotte. During the reign of King Devanampiya Tissa, in 247 BC, Buddhism was introduced in me by Arahat Mahendra, the son of Emperor Ashoka of India. My many nicknames include Serendib, Teardrop of India, Resplendent Isle, Island of Dharma and Pearl of the Orient.

Sri Lanka

According to *Time* magazine (9 February 1998), "If there is any place on earth which resembles a paradise, it may be Sri Lanka." Peace talks brought about a one-month ceasefire between the Liberation Tigers of Tamil Eelam (LTTE) and the government from 24 December 2001 (the first in seven years), which was renewed in January 2002. The two have been at loggerhead for long.

Glossary

P. 1

Pietra dura: Mosaic work using semi-precious stones.

P. 2

Guy de Maupassant: He is considered to be the greatest French short story writer. Some of his stories include: *Une Vie* (A Woman's Life), *Bel Ami, Pierre Et Jean*, and *Le Horla.*
Seurat: Georges Seurat was a 19th-century French painter, known for his technique of portraying the play of light using tiny brushstrokes of contrasting colours. This is called 'pointillism'.
Douanier Rousseau: He was a customs inspector (*douanier*) and became a painter after his retirement.

P. 4

Samarkand: Samarkand is in Uzbekistan. It was the city of Tamerlane or Timur the lame.

P. 5

Royal Collection: This is one of the finest art collections in the world and held in trust by the Queen as Sovereign for her successors and the nation. The collection is on display at the main royal residences and is shown in a programme of special exhibitions and through loans to institutions in the world.
Rembrandt: Dutch painter and engraver, 1606-1669
Rubens: Flemish painter, 1577-1640.
Vermeer: Jan or Johannes Vermeer van Delft was a Dutch painter, 1632-1675. Most of his work portrays figures in interiors.
Poussin: Nicolas Poussin was a French painter, 1594-1665.
Canova: One of the greatest Italian sculptors of modern times, 1757-1822.
Mews: A row of houses that are converted from stables.
Coronation: The ceremony of crowning a sovereign or a sovereign's consort.
Changing of Guard: The proper name of the ceremony known as 'Changing the Guard' is actually guard mounting. This is one of the oldest royal ceremonies of Britain — a new guard exchange duty with the old guard. The handover is accompanied by a guards band. Guard Mounting takes place in the forecourt of Buckingham Place at 11.30 a.m. and lasts for about 45 minutes. There is no Guard Mounting in very wet weather. During autumn and winter, Guard Mounting takes place on alternate dates.

P. 6

Mantee: A small or verandah outside the upper floors.
Gold leaf: Gold that has been beaten into very thin sheets to use for gilding.

P. 7
Stupa: A dome-shaped Buddhist shrine.
Balustrade: A railing supported by short pillars.

P. 8
Achaemenids: A clan of the Persians. The Achaemenid Empire came to an end when Alexander the Great defeated the army of the last ruler and moved on to Susa and Persepolis to loot the vast royal treasures.

P. 9
Pulpit: A raised platform in a church from which a preacher delivers a sermon.
Minarets: A slender tower with a balcony on top, usually seen in mosques.
Havelis and kothis: Mansions and large houses.

P. 11
Poush: A month of the Bengali calendar, usually from 17 December to 15 January.
Frescoes: Paintings done in water colour on wet plaster on walls or ceiling.
Murals: Paintings done on walls.

P. 12
Gerbil: A mouse-like animal found in dry areas of Africa and Asia.
Jerboa: A rodent (mouse-like creature) that stays in the desert. It has very long legs that enable it to jump.
Cape hare: The long ears and black-and-white tail is most obvious in flight. It is distinguished from the scrub hare by being smaller in stature and the absence of pure white underparts.

P. 13
Gopurams: A temple gate that usually has five to seven storeys.
Shiva: The Hindu God, who is also called 'the destroyer' among the trinity of Vishnu-Shiva-Brahma.
Mandapam: A shrine or platform for auspicious rites and events.

P. 14
Pentelic marble: Found in Greece, it is pure white and of very fine grain. The marble is quarried from the Pentelic mountain range, just north of Athens, in Attica.
Chryselephantine: Statues that were built up on a wooden core, with ivory representing the flesh and gold, the clothes. The two most known examples are the statue of Athena in the Parthenon and of Zeus in the a temple at Olympia.

P. 15
Guillotine: A machine with a blade that moves up and down and is used for beheading people.

Electric chair: A chair in which criminals are killed by electric shock.
Hertford Gaol: Gaol is a different way of spelling 'jail'. This particular one is in use in west-central England; it is attached to Hertford Castle.

P. 16
Molluscs: Invertebrates, usually with soft bodies and an external shell, like the snails and slugs.
Algae: A very simple green plant.
Fringing reefs: A coral reef that lies close to the shore.
Coral cays: A low bank or reef made up of corals.

P. 17
Pristine: Pure.
Ancillary: Extension, part or an annexe.

P. 19
Viharas: Viharas are the dwelling places donated to the normally wandering Buddhist monks.
Vishnu: The principal Hindu God of the trinity Shiva-Vishnu-Brahma.
Lakshmi: The wife of Vishnu and the Hindu Goddess of Wealth.
Garuda: The bird which carried Vishnu.

P. 20
Shivalinga: Linga means 'sign, mark or symbol'. *Shivalinga* is basically an emblem of Lord Shiva. It is usually made of stone but can also be of wood, metal, crystal and soapstone.
Narasimha: An incarnation of Lord Vishnu and in which he appears as a half-lion and half-man.

P. 21
Façade: The front of a building.
Cornucopia: The horn of plenty. A mythological goat-horn that provides an unlimited supply of flowers, fruit and corn.

P. 23
Nagari: An early form of the Devanagari script, which is still used in modern Indian languages.

P. 24
Trellised: A light metal, stone or wooden framework, usually used as a support.

P. 25
Guarani: The term *Guarani* has been used in at least three different ways. First, it refers to the language spoken by a large group of people who inhabited vast

areas of southern Brazil, Uruguay and Argentine. It is also used to denote the culture of the American Indians who speak the Guarani language. Also, the native Indians who converted to Christianity and became known as Guarani, while those who avoided conversion became known as Cayua or Caingua, which means 'men of the forest'.

P. 26
Aswan granite: Pink and red granite quarried in Aswan, Egypt. It is known for it rigidity and stiffness.
Sacrophagus: A stone coffin.

P. 27
Venetian chandelier: A particular variety, probably the best of the chandeliers. It is made in Venice, usually by hand-blown fine glasses.
Osler chandelier: Chandeliers made by F & C Osler, established in Birmingham, UK, in 1807. They were renowned for the size and elaborate design of their creations.

P. 28
Baroque: A style of European art, architecture and music of the 17th and 18th centuries. It is characterised by the highly elaborate and ornate style.
Manuline: An ornate Portuguese style seen during the 15th and 16th centuries.
Laterite: A reddish clayey material which becomes hard when dried and is used as building material in some regions.
Transept: In churches that are shaped like a cross, the central long section is called the nave and the arms are called transepts.
Thanedar: In India, a person in charge of the local police station or prison.
Belfry: The place where bells are kept in a bell tower of a church or chapel.
Sacristy: A room in a church where things needed for worship are kept and where a priest prepares for prayers or service.
Franciscan friar: A friar is a man belonging to a certain religious order, especially the Augustinian, Carmelite, Dominican, and Franciscan orders. The Franciscans follow the rules laid by St. Francis of Assisi.
Consecrated: To be made or declared sacred or holy.
Our Lady of Miracles: A form of the Virgin Mary.
Insignia: A distinguishing badge or sign.
Tabernacle: An ornamented cabinet in a church where holy water or consecrated bread may be kept.
Evangelist: A person who seeks to convert others to Christianity by preaching.

P. 32
Canonisation: A declaration of a dead person as a saint by the Roman Catholic church.
Norman Abbey: A place occupied by monks or nuns and built in Normandy or by the Normans.

Cathedral: The main church in a diocese. A diocese is the area under the religious care of a Bishop.
Parish church: A church of a very small administrative zone, called parish.
Sacrament: A religious ceremony like baptism, where a person is included into Christianity formally. Sacrament also denotes the holy objects connected to a religious ceremony in a church, like the holy water and holy bread.

P. 33
Nagara: The ancient Indian texts on architecture classify temples into three different orders: the Nagara style followed by temples in northern India, the Dravidian or southern style, and the Vesara or hybrid style. The Orissan temples in Khajuraho style are characteristic of the Nagara style.
Shaivism: A sect of Hinduism that worships and focuses on Lord Shiva as the main deity.
Vaishnavism: A sect of Hinduism that worships and focuses on Lord Vishnu as the main deity.
Tantrism: A form of Hinduism that developed in the 4th and 5th centuries BC that focused primarily on ritualistic magic and power. Lord Shiva and the Mother Goddess are usually the main deities for people who follow this sect.

P. 35
Porphyry: A fine igneous rock that typically has a reddish mass with crystals of feldspar.
Brunelleschi: A sculptor and architect of Florence, 1377-1446.
Arcades: A covered passage with arches along one or both sides.
Julio-Claudian family: A stream of Roman emperors, who ruled from 27 BC until AD 68. These men were Augustus, Tiberius, Gaius (better known as Caligula), Claudius and Nero.

P. 37
Raptors: Birds of prey like vultures, eagles, etc.

P. 38
Mahajanapada: Major states in early India.
Krishna: An incarnation of Lord Vishnu and the most popular Hindu God.

P. 39
Austerlitz: The battle of Austerlitz is regarded as Napoleon Bonaparte's greatest victory, in which he destroyed the armies of Russia and Austria.
Piers: The pillar of an arch or that supporting a bridge.
Bas reliefs: Relief work is a method of carving in which the design is raised from the surface. Bas relief is lesser or low relief.
Armistice Day: Also known as Veteran's Day; it is celebrated on November 11 as

the anniversary of the peace treaty which was signed in the Forest of Compiegne by the Allies and Germans in 1918, ending the First World War, after four years of conflict.
Place de L'Etoile: An area in Paris.

P. 40
Gladiator: A man trained to fight with weapons or bare hands with other men or wild animals in an arena.
Amphitheatre: A round space with seats around a central space where people can see dramatic events.

P. 42
Ibises: Ibises belong to the same order of birds as herons, storks and flamingoes.
Spoonbill: A common name for a large wading bird related to the ibis. The common spoonbill of Europe, Asia and Africa, *Platalea leucorodia*, is white and crested.
Cormorant: A sea bird.
Paddybirds: Small birds; also called Java sparrows.

P. 45
Papacy: The authority of the Pope or the period of authority of a Pope.
Ponte Vecchio: The oldest and most famous bridge in Florence, built by Taddeo Gaddi.
Duomo: The cathedral of Florence that involved over six centuries of work. Its basic design was by Arnolfo di Cambio at the end of the 13th century. It was given the name of Santa Maria del Fiore (Hoy Mary of Flower) in 1412.
Uffizi Gallery: One of the richest European museums in Florence.
Piazza della Signoria: A central square of Florence. It has been the political centre of Florence for centuries.
Medici chapels: A personal sepulchre of the Medici family. The work was started by Michelangelo and completed by his students after his departure to Rome.

P. 46
Aborigine: A term that denotes the original or native people of a particular place, especially in Australia.
Wharfing: A wharf is an area where ships are attached for loading or unloading.
Quay: A platform alongside water or projecting into water for loading and unloading of ships.

P. 54
Palatine chapel: A chapel built by an unknown architect at Aachen, Germany. It was founded in 1132 by Ruggero II and was consecrated to St. Peter. It is incorporated within Aachen Cathedral, which was added to UNESCO's World Heritage List in 1978.

Transenna: A marble screen.
Mass: The service of Christian worship in which wine and bread are consecrated and shared.
Old covenant: Old Hebrew or Jewish law that existed before the coming of Jesus Christ. It is a biblical approach in which its followers believe and who worship Jesus Christ.
Mosaic law: The 10 commandments of the old covenant set by Moses before the coming of Christ.

P. 57
Lapis lazuli: A bright blue metamorphic rock.
Jadeite: A form of jade; a white, blue or green silicate material.

P. 58
Corridors: Regular paths through which wild animals, especially elephants, move in herds.
Giant lobelia: A flowering plant found in the mountains of eastern Africa. The point where the plant grows is protected by young leaves. After a period of 30-70 years, a large, cylindrical mass of small flowers (this is called an inflorescence) is formed. The plant then dies. The dark green leaves form an enclosing circle of up to 50 cm in diameter, which opens during the day and closes by night to resemble a cabbage-head.

P.59
Baisakhi: A spring harvest festival celebrated in Punjab.

P. 61
Escarpment: A steep slope at the edge of a plateau.
Dolostone: A rock with dolomite, a mineral consisting mainly of carbonate of calcium or magnesium.
Shale: A sedimentary rock made from clay or mud.

P. 62
Eutrophication: The overgrowth of plants in a water body due to excessive fertilisers, which deplete the water body of dissolved oxygen and kill the fish and other water organisms.

P.68
Crustaceans: A group of aquatic Arthropoda that include crabs, lobsters and shrimps.

P.69
Coatis: Raccoon-like mammals, a member of the Procyonidae family. Coatis have reddish brown fur, which is lighter on their undersides. Their ankles are

double jointed, allowing them to descend trees with their head first. Their nose is long and pointed, with an extremely flexible tip.
Montezuma oropendolas: Birds that live in the rain-forest regions near water and clearings, but not too deep in the forest. They are characterised by their nests that dangle like stockings.

P.71
Mahashivaratri: A major festival of Lord Shiva celebrated on the 14th day of Magh. A fast is observed on this day and devotees throng the temples.
Jyotirlinga: Lord Shiva is supposed to have first manifested himself as a *jyotirlinga* or *linga* of light. There are supposed to be 12 *jyotirlingas* on the earth.

P. 74
Petroglyphs: A rock carving.

P. 76
Capital: A pillar.

P. 78
Korai: Sculpted marble statues of young Greek women created between the 7th and 5th centuries BC.

P. 81
Mandala: Mandala in Sanskrit language stands for a circle, polygon, community or connection.

P. 82
Bluestone: A bluish or grey building stone; a dolorite stone.
Sarsen: A silified sandstone boulder.
Lintel: A horizontal support across a door or window.

P. 86
Sea-level canal and lock canal: A lock canal is that in which gates are present at each end, built into a canal or river for the purpose of raising or lowering a vessel from the water. A sea-level canal is an open canal.

P. 89
GPS satellite: A Global Positioning System satellite.
North Col and North Ridge: Col is a Welsh word, which means 'saddle'. The North Col is the low point of North Ridge, one of the three great ridges that emanate from the summit of Mount Everest.

P. 92
Edo period: Japanese period between 1603-1867; also Edo is another name for Tokyo.

Samurai: A Japanese warrior.

P. 94
Khmer: An ancient Cambodian kingdom; it is also the official language of Cambodia.
Citadel: A fortress protecting or dominating a city.
Laterite: See 28.

P. 98
Catenary: A catenary is the shape that a chain or necklace forms when held by the two ends. The Dutch mathematician Christiaan Huygens named this curve from the Latin word catenarius, which means 'related to a chain'. The equation for a catenary curve is: y = k cosh (x/k), where cosh is the hyperbolic cosine {cosh (x)=(ex + e-x)/2) and k is the y-intercept where the curve hits the y-axis}.

P. 99
Hieroglyphic: Writing comprising a stylised picture of a sound, word or a syllable.